Arizona Gunfire

Chet Cunningham

WHEELER PUBLISHING
An imprint of Thomson Gale, a part of The Thomson Corporation

THOMSON
━━━━━✳━━━━━™
GALE

Detroit • New York • San Francisco • New Haven, Conn. • Waterville, Maine • London

THOMSON
GALE
™

Copyright © 1980 by American Art Enterprises.
Chisholm Series.
Thomson Gale is part of The Thomson Corporation.
Thomson and Star Logo and Wheeler are trademarks and Gale is a registered trademark used herein under license.

LIBRARY OF CONGRESS CATALOGING-IN-PUBLICATION DATA

Cunningham, Chet.
   Arizona gunfire / by Chet Cunningham.
     p. cm. — (Chisholm series) (Wheeler Publishing large print Western)
   ISBN-13: 978-1-59722-451-2 (pbk. : alk. paper)
   ISBN-10: 1-59722-451-0 (pbk. : alk. paper) 1. Large type books. I. Title.
PS3553.U468A89 2007
813'.54—dc22   2006035322

Published in 2007 by arrangement with Chet Cunningham.

Printed in the United States of America on permanent paper
10 9 8 7 6 5 4 3 2 1

ARIZONA GUNFIRE

This Large Print Book carries the
Seal of Approval of N.A.V.H.

Arizona Gunfire

CHAPTER 1
BLOOD IN THE
MORNING

August, 1872, Arizona Territory
Wade Chisholm had taken three days instead of the usual two to ride the sixty miles from Prescott to the village of Phoenix outside the Superstition Mountains. There had been no rush. He had finished his report on the Salt River Gorge Cave patrol for Col. George Crook and now was free of the army for a while. He would go back and work for them again as a scout, but not for a while.

Chisholm eased up to the hitching rail in front of the McCurdy General Store at about ten that morning before the sun was at its hottest. He wiped sweat from his forehead. His shirt was soaked through with perspiration and his horse, tired but sound. As he stepped off the mount, passerbys realized that he was over six feet tall, dark and lean with a touch of anger around his face when he wasn't smiling.

He pulled off his brown, high-crowned hat and slapped it against his pants and shirt, dislodging as much of the trail dust as he could before he stepped on the wooden porch of the store. His face was clean shaven. The wind and sun had weathered it, showing that he had spent more days and nights outside than he did under a roof.

Dark eyes relaxed a little as he headed for the door and pulled it open.

There was no blur of blue dress, no soft pretty girl rushing to meet him. Just Josh McCurdy looking up against the sudden splash of sunlight through the door. He and Josh had been good friends for five years.

"Oh, it's you, Chisholm. Forgot that red hair of yours got dyed a little to brown. How the hell are you?"

"Tolerable, Josh . . . and you?"

"Getting by. If you're looking for Hannah, she ain't been in yet today. Probably didn't feel well this morning. I figured on going over to have a look at her come noon time."

A sudden chill filtered through Chisholm's body and he gripped his hat a little tighter.

"Well, why don't I save you the trip. I'll just ride on over there and take a look." He turned and reached for the door.

"Come back this afternoon, we got to talk. Chisholm, I went back to the ranch Hannah's folks tried to start. Thought I might find something the Indians had missed when they burned them out couple of weeks back. And I found something I want you to take a look at. It could be important."

"Yeah, Josh, I'll be back." He closed the front door and ran to his horse, in a rush now. Unexplained, but gnawing at him, came a sudden feeling of dread, of pain, of loss. He rode at a gallop the three hundred yards down the dirt street and around the corner to the small blue-trimmed, white-painted house and stopped at the front door. Nothing looked unusual. She must have been tired this morning and overslept. Hannah oversleep?

He dropped the mount's reins on the ground and took long strides to the door where he knocked sharply four times. There was no sound from inside as he waited.

A shiver thundered down his spine and Wade Chisholm's face twisted into a frown. He knocked again. The house wasn't that large, it wouldn't take that much time. . . . He saw the horses' hoofprints near the small porch and stared at it. It wasn't like any shoe he had seen. And what was it doing so close to the porch?

He twisted the knob and pushed at the door. It was locked. Locked? There was no cause to lock your door in Phoenix where everyone knew everyone else. He pushed at it again, then rushed around the side of the house to the back door. Wade was sure it didn't have a lock.

Chisholm rammed the door inward and dashed into the small kitchen. There was no fire, the kitchen had been used but not cleaned, which was not like Hannah. He started into the small living room when he saw the trail of drops of blood on the floor.

A cold resolve fastened on him and wouldn't let go. Wade put his emotions aside and followed the blood trail. The living room was dishevelled. One chair had been tipped over, a picture had fallen off the wall, the curtains were tightly pulled closed.

The blood led to the bedroom. Wade hesitated at the closed door, then kicked the door open, his six gun in hand and leveled straight ahead.

Hannah lay on the bed, naked, not moving. He knew Hannah Miller was dead. In the past few years he had seen too many dead bodies not to know. One hand covered her crotch as if in protection and protest. The blood had come from her hand but that hadn't killed her.

Wade choked back a sob, losing part of his control as he neared the bed. The covers were rumpled, her face locked in anguish, brown hair partly covering one shoulder. One breast had been burned three times with a cigar or cigarette.

Then he saw why her hand had bled. Her little finger on the left hand had been cut off, neatly severed at the joint. The cut off part was missing. He saw the white and purple marks on Hannah's throat where strong hands had strangled the life from her. Chisholm found scratches on her thighs and her stomach. She had been raped, then strangled. Who would do such a thing?

Chisholm sagged. He sat upon the bed, reeling with the injustice of it, the wanton killing, the terrible suffering she had endured. For five minutes, he let his rage build, letting the hatred for her assaulters grow, develop and build into an unforgettable fury that was now such a part of him that it would need to be burned out before he could be rid of it.

He slashed tears away from his eyes as he stood. Then he methodically checked the room. On the bedroom floor he found a cigar band. Few persons in the west smoked cigars; they cost too much. It was a red band with a white circle and the words "Red Dot Cigar." Chisholm put it in the pocket of his buckskin vest and kept searching. He

11

found nothing else in the bedroom, then looked over the living room and kitchen. There was nothing that didn't belong there.

Outside he went over the ground carefully. With the stub of a pencil he sketched the pattern of the horse shoes he found near the front porch, and more at the back door. There were two that were distinctive. The first was a regular shoe with a sturdy inch-wide section at each side of the open end. It was as if the metal had been added for support. The second one was a poorly made shoe, or it had been bent. It formed more of a "V" than a regular "U" horseshoe and should be easy to track.

He rode to Josh McCurdy's store, took a bottle of whiskey off the shelf and pulled the cork.

"Wade, what's the matter, you look furious, deadly."

Chisholm tipped the bottle and drank in long swallows until he had to breathe. Then he lowered the bottle gasping for air. He handed the bottle back to McCurdy. "Josh, Hannah is dead. She's been raped and strangled. Last night is my guess. There were two or three, perhaps even four men, hoof prints all around the house. You take care of Hannah for me, I'm going after the killers."

"Dead? But just last night . . . she was here."

"You tend to the funeral, Josh. I want some supplies. Jerky, coffee, some more rounds for my Spencer and my Colt. Might throw in an extra blanket and a tin can to boil coffee. It could be a long ride."

"Where to, any idea?"

"It's a vengeance ride, Josh, it could go anywhere and be for months on end. I won't be back until whoever killed Hannah is dead — dead with as much anger and pain as I can deliver."

"Now, Wade. We've got some law. . . ."

"*Some* law, but not much. I won't get in the law's way. You have the sheriff take a look. Where's that jerky and the ammunition? They've probably got twelve hours head start on me already."

Chisholm checked at the hotel on his way out of town, but no one had seen two or three strange men in town the day before. The two bars had served no strangers for two days.

He hadn't expected it to be easy. Back at Hannah's house he rode around the building slowly at a hundred yards, and on the second trip he picked up prints of two horses heading north, moving fast. There

13

was no way to identify the shoes, not when they were running so hard. But he would find a place later when the pair slowed. He followed the tracks. There seemed to be no attempt to disguise the trail or to throw off a tracker. He watched the route for half an hour, determined that they were heading toward the far bend of the Salt River. He opened up his big black mount, gambling that they didn't change their heading and raced hard for the bend in the Salt. He trailed along the near bank of the now dry stream for two hundred yards before he cut the trail again.

Now there were three horses, and in the soft sand he found both tracks he had seen before, the U shaped shoe with the reinforcing, and the V-type shoe. The riders had evidently met at or near that point. They had stood there for sometime, and one had thrown down a brown paper cigarette stub.

Chisholm dismounted, picked up the burned out butt and put it in a small envelope in his saddle bags. He sniffed the tobacco, but could tell little from it except it was cheap and redder than most he had seen. There was nothing else on the ground to help him.

He mounted and followed the tracks. They paralleled the dry stream bed until they came to another bend where a shallow pool of water had collected. The men had watered their horses here, and so did Chisholm, then he crossed the stream with the tracks and angled with them north and northwest. Prescott was the only town up that way, unless they were going all the way to Flagstaff. The tracks showed that the riders did not now seem to be in a hurry. Another half mile and he found where they had camped for the night. A small fire had been built and coffee brewed. He found the dumped out grounds, and two empty tin cans that had contained sliced peaches.

Cowhands on the search for work? Bad time of the year for range work. Surely they were not professional outlaws. They seemed too unsophisticated in their movements for that. Or were they just three young men out for a night on the town? He didn't know, he didn't care; they would die, all die, slowly, painfully.

Chisholm rode on. The trail angled north and he stopped to examine some shoots of grass and weeds the riders had crossed. Most of the grass had sprung up after the hoofprints had flattened it. He estimated that the men were now only five hours ahead of him.

For his noon meal, Chisholm chewed on

some jerky and had a few swallows of water. He would soon be taking only two meals a day, and then Indian style, one meal. If his horse could hold out he should catch them before they got to Prescott.

On the first small rise he checked the direction of the tracks. Prescott must be their destination. They might swing out to stop at the Henshaw ranch, but only if they knew it was there. As he rode he tried to outguess them. Would they stop at Henshaws? At first he figured they would go straight through to Prescott, have their horses reshod and be moving again without sleep.

Then he reversed his reasoning. They would find the Henshaw place, rest and eat there. They were not as tough as he figured them to be. After Prescott they would strike out for Flagstaff or perhaps Denver. They didn't seem to be hardened killers, either they were new at death or they had panicked. He had three more hours to make up his mind.

It was late in the afternoon and four miles from the Henshaw ranch when he decided to gamble. He would go through the Rancho ravine and over East Butte in a short cut to save three miles by the trail. If the killers had hit Henshaws he would find out, if not he had lost only two miles. Every mile saved counted now.

He arrived at the Henshaw ranchhouse about four that afternoon, tired and dusty. Mrs. Henshaw was surprised to see him back so soon.

"My men are out on the range, trying to find some cattle they thought ran off," she said. She was a big woman, almost six feet tall with wide shoulders, the sturdy type of pioneer woman needed for Arizona.

She nodded when he asked about three riders.

"Matter of fact I fed them just a little after noon. Said they was cowhands up from Texas looking for work. I told them they better sashay back to Kansas, that's where the beef are. We just raise coyotes, rattlesnakes and road runners up here."

"Can you describe the men for me, Mrs. Henshaw?"

She had insisted that he come in for some pumpkin pie and some left over stew she heated up. The pumpkins weren't keeping this year as well as they usually did, so she had to cook this one. The pie was delicious.

"Well, one of them was a little feller, not more than five-feet three, maybe four. He had a thin face and wore eyeglasses and kept

17

sniffing all the time like he had a cold. Said he always did that, something about the air didn't agree with him. Can you imagine that?"

"No, ma'am, I certainly can't."

"Well the other gent was tall, big as you. Wore cowboy gear and a gun tied down low. He had a mean look about him and seemed nervous. He didn't talk much, just a howdy and a goodbye. He had a black beard and black hair, but no eyebrows at all. That was strange, no eyebrows, but a moustache and all."

She ate half a piece of pie and then nodded. "The third man seemed to be the ramrod. He was taller than the little one, but not as big as the tall one. Never took off his hat, but I saw some brownish hair. Long sideburns and all. He had a scar too, down from one corner of his mouth. Left side, I guess. About an inch long, still he was a good looking one."

"Did you hear any names?"

"Just once. The little man called one of them Hart. And he got a look that would kill. No other names. They lit out from here about four hours ago. You the law? They in some kind of trouble?"

"They're in trouble, and I'm the only kind of law them gents are going to need."

The woman grinned, showing crooked teeth. "You sound like my Will. Us Henshaws like that kind of talk. Got to protect your own out here in the wilderness."

He finished the coffee, thanked her, and moved out at a pace he knew he couldn't expect the horse to keep up for long, but it would be dark soon. He doubted if the riders would go the other thirty miles into Prescott tonight. They had traveled a long ways and would be tired. He could catch them if they camped when darkness hit. For him it wasn't a matter of tracking them anymore. It was simply staying on the main trail to Prescott or near it, watching and listening.

He slowed when darkness fell. He was puzzled. The trio had acted like they didn't expect anyone to follow them. Why? Or were they confident enough to think they could handle anyone who tried to take them?

Chisholm slowed again as the darkness deepened. His eyes adjusted to the pale moonlight. He came to a small rise and paused. He looked ahead to the north and northwest but no where did he see the glow of a campfire. That would have made it too easy.

For another hour he moved slowly along the moonlit trail, staying on the track, watching, listening. But an hour later it was his nose that picked up the first taint of smoke in the silent, crisp night air. The smoke came from his right, off the trail and up a good sized watercourse. Chisholm stopped and left his horse well off the trail, decided not to take his Spencer rifle with him. He left his hat and vest, slid the knife into a scabbard on his right leg, and wished he had brought his long knife across his back. Chisholm checked the loads in his six gun and the extra rounds in his pocket, then moved up the draw as silently as an Apache, making sure he was down wind from his victims and taking satisfaction that he had caught them so easily. He slid around a boulder in the wash and looked up stream fifty yards at a small cooking fire. Three shapes moved around the blaze.

Chisholm took out his blade and checked its sharpness. He felt he was 100% Apache Chiricahua as he moved up silently on the men using every Indian trick he knew.

CHAPTER 2
SCREAM IN THE
NIGHT

For a moment he was twelve again, sneaking up on his Chiricahua playmates, stalking the bigger, older boys who had ridiculed him, teased and taunted him until he had learned their games better than they and out-thought and out-stalked them at every turn. Only now it was no game. He crawled on his hands and knees along the dry wash, making absolutely no sound, moving dry sticks, listening to the growing sound of the men's voices ahead. One spoke in a high whine, a second's voice was heavy but casual. The third voice when it came was sharp, commanding, and Chisholm recognized the ring of military authority in it.

He peered around a rock which the rains had washed free of soil where it stood in the middle of the wash. The night air had cooled as the trail moved upward. They were slightly west of the main string of mountains with Antelope Peak still ahead and East of them, but the air was far different from that of the desert flatlands around Phoenix. The men sat close to the fire, cooking, and he saw them roasting a chicken on a spit over the flames. They probably had stolen it on the way out of the Henshaw ranch.

He wasn't interested in the fried chicken. He was concerned with the positioning of the men. How should he attack? Instinctively, his Chiricahua blood and mind surfaced, and he knew where and when to strike.

The time was not now, but after they went to sleep leaving perhaps one man on guard. And that man would be the small one with the eye glasses and the whine for a voice because the other two were stronger than he. So the small man would die first, then the biggest one because of his physical threat, and the leader would be last. But before they died, Chisholm determined, each would talk. Each would admit his part in the murder, then beg for mercy and grovel and suffer, then die. With these animals he could utilize all of his Chiricahua savagery, making them beg for a quick death, and still he would not think he had done enough to repay them for the brutal rape-death of Hannah Miller.

Wade Chisholm lay in the wash waiting. He did not move for two hours, not until the bird was cooked, eaten, the jokes told, some whiskey drank and the fire put out. They went to sleep quickly and to his surprise no one was left on guard. Strange, Chisholm thought as he moved closer to the camp, then swung around to the far side to come directly upon the small man. Vengeance swirled in his brain as Chisholm moved silently, slowly toward his victim.

As he moved he remembered his father, a huge man with flaming red hair. His father who had come into the Apache nation as a tall, powerful ghost, suddenly walking into the inner camp of the Chiricahua fully armed and without being seen by a single Apache scout. He gave his rifle and pistol to a squaw, ignored the shouts and threats of the embarrassed Chiricahua braves, and walked boldly to the chief's tent, sat down beside him, produced a short pipe and smoked. The action was so bold, so brave and heroic, that the chief made Big Jim Chisholm an Apache blood brother and gave him total freedom to travel and live in Apache lands. He was not a warrior he told them, but a prospector.

They laughed at him. A man who hunted the useless metal known as squaw's clay that the round-eyes called gold. It was stupid. But they did not laugh when he challenged them to their own games, wrestling, running, knife and axe throwing. He beat them at all their games except the short bow, and he wasn't far behind there. The Indians called him Big Red Hair.

Shortly after that he took as his squaw Blue Feather, a young and beautiful girl of fourteen who soon gave birth to a son. They called him Little Red Hair since he was all Apache except for the flaming red hair inherited from his father. Three years later Big Jim Chisholm was ambushed and killed by a Chiricahua Big Jim had disgraced and had caused to leave the camp.

When Little Red Hair was twelve, he was captured in a surprise raid by a patrol of U.S. Cavalry. During the raid, Blue Feather lost her life. The troopers killed all the braves and all but a few of the children and squaws. Since Little Red Hair was obviously different, he was taken and raised by a friendly army officer who moved around to various forts and camps in the west. The boy was known to have the last name Chisholm, and his new parents named him Wade. He was quick and bright. At school he soon knew more than the teacher. After several tries he received an appointment to

West Point and four years later came home as an officer and a gentleman.

After three years of service in the Army, he resigned his commission, but he couldn't stay away from the west. He became a scout for the army in the Arizona Territory.

Now, moving up silently on the sleeping round-eyes, he wondered how a West Point graduate could contemplate the slow murder of three men who had raped and strangled a beautiful young girl. He abruptly pushed that thought aside; it was round-eye thinking. Now he was an Apache! A deadly Chiricahua, and the three men sleeping would soon be screaming for mercy in atonement for their brutal murder.

Chisholm crawled up on the sleeping man slowly, testing the air, watching all three men, making sure all were sleeping. One had a pistol near his hand. Chisholm moved it, silently. Then he smashed his hand into the small man's throat, and at once clamped his hand over the man's mouth so he could not scream. He waited a moment as the man struggled. He glanced at the others. Neither man moved. Chisholm picked up the small man, put him over his shoulder and walked silently up the dry wash for five hundred yards.

He lay the man on the ground and stared

at him. He indeed was the one with the whining voice, the eye glasses and the sniffling nose. The man's windpipe had not been crushed, only bruised and it took several more minutes before he could talk. When his throat was back to normal, the man saw moonlight glint off the knife that brushed his throat.

"I want answers and I want them now, or I'll slit your throat," Chisholm said, his voice low, threatening. "What's your name?"

"Harry Carlyle. Who are you?"

"I'm the man who's going to tkill you if you don't keep on talking. Who are the two men with you, their names?"

"I don't think I should. . . ."

The point of Chisholm's knife drove half an inch between Harry Carlyle's ribs in his back and he flinched and screamed.

"What the hell?"

"The next time it goes in an inch, into your lung. What are the names?"

"Horst Berger, he's the big one. The other guy is Shipley Hart. Christ, keep that knife away from me."

"Hart, he's your leader?"

"Yeah. We was both with him during the war. On the wrong side, the Gray. He was our sergeant, and we just kind of tailed along after we were mustered out."

"That was seven years ago."

"Time goes fast."

"Hannah Miller," Chisholm said and watched the man cringe, then his eyes went wide in terror.

"Hey, I didn't have nothing to do with that. Nothing. All I did was hold the horses and then inside. Inside . . . I watched."

"But you didn't try to stop them, did you?"

"No sir, they'd have shot me."

"Where are you headed?"

"Hart said Flagstaff, then maybe Denver, maybe San Francisco. Hart is getting tired of this dry country."

"Flag, he'll never make it."

"Mister, you got to let me go. I didn't do nothing. I never hurt the girl."

"You never tried to help her. What happened?"

"Look, I told them to leave her alone. She wasn't some girl in a remote ranch house. We was coming into town and we seen her leave the store, must have been about supper time. So we watched her go to that little house and we come up behind it, walking. Left our horses out by that bunch of mesquite. We slipped up and knocked on the back door. She opened it up and Hart walked in with his six gun drawn. Then he

27

made her cook us supper. Afterwards Hart got fooling around with her. Nothing he planned. It just happened. He put his hand on her breast and squeezed and she slapped him. Hart slapped her back. Then he grabbed her blouse and tore it open.

"Hart laughed and tore more of it away. He slapped her and ripped off more of her clothes. He just kept hitting her and ripping off clothes until she was crying and didn't have a thing on.

"He chased her into the bedroom and slammed the door and I heard her yelling. He came out about an hour later and Berger went in. When he came out we left there fast and rode into the darkness. I got scared and lost, but then I found them at the river. So help me, mister, I never touched her."

"Who cut off her finger, Hart?"

"Cut her finger . . . I don't know what you're saying."

"Who strangled her?"

"Strangled . . . oh, my God! That had to be Berger. He was with her last. I never knew. I'd never kill a woman, so help me!"

Chisholm knelt across from the small man where he sat in the sand.

"Harry, I believe you. I think you've told me the truth. But the verdict is still guilty. You're just as guilty of the rape and strangulation of Hannah Miller as the other two. The sentence is the same as for them. It's death, Harry."

Before Harry Carlyle could say a word, Chisholm rammed the six inch hunting knife forward, plunged it between ribs. The sharp point pierced flesh, muscle and slashed through Harry's heart. He was dead before Chisholm pulled out the blade. He pushed Harry away from him, wiped the blade on the man's pants and stood.

He ran lightly back down the draw toward where he had left the other two sleeping men. He moved with absolute silence as before, but when he came to the spot where the fire had been, he found only a few glowing coals. The two men who had been sleeping were gone. Nothing was left, not a pan or a blanket. Chisholm had not spotted the horses the men used, but he was sure they were gone now, too. For whatever reason, the men had awakened, or perhaps one had been awake all the time and let him take Harry.

Why hadn't the one awake simply killed the intruder with a well placed pistol shot? Chisholm could not figure it out. Instead he accepted what he knew for a fact and ran back down the draw to where he had left his horse and equipment. Everything was as he had left it. He put on his vest and hat, wiped the knife again and put it back in his scabbard, and mounted the black.

The men wouldn't ride far tonight in the darkness. They might not even head for Prescott now, but it was point of departure for other trails. Yes, they probably would go to Prescott after all, but he would be there first.

Chisholm settled his big black down to a steady walk along the trail as they slid through the darkness. By dawn he could be half way to Prescott. Wade would decide if he wanted to find a spot to trap the men. It depended on the layout of the land and which trail they took. For a few moments he was afraid that Hart and Berger had been frightened and would turn and run the other way. Then he remembered Hart's voice. Such a man would step aside for no one. He would carry out his plan and if anyone got in his way, that man would be eliminated. At least Hart would try. But this time Wade Chisholm would be the one blocking Hart's desires.

After midnight the black began making noises like she wanted some rest. Chisholm figured he had traveled at least ten miles in the darkness which should put him far ahead of Hart and Berger. He led the black up a narrow arroyo with a few trees and tied her to a bush, then wrapped up in his blanket and settled down on the ground.

As he was drifting off to sleep, Wade kept reminding himself that he would wake up at daylight. If he thought about it enough he would wake up automatically.

A squirrel chattered in a pine tree to his left when Jim opened his eyes. It was morning and well after daybreak. He couldn't see the sun, but he knew he was late. Quickly he got his gear together, rolled his blanket and tied it behind his saddle, then took a big chaw of jerky and a swallow of water. When he tightened the cinch strap on the saddle, the black complained.

He gave it an extra tug, stepped into the leather and rode.

When he came to the Prescott trail at the bottom of the ravine, he checked carefully for tracks. He didn't see any that had the shoe markings he had been following on and off, so he turned up the trail and moved toward Prescott.

If the pair got to the small town before he did, it would be bad. He could not afford to be involved in a shoot out with either man, or chance anything that would bring charges by the law. Anything he did with Hart and Berger had to be done out here somewhere,

31

in the wilderness where his own gun and blade would be the only law of the land, and where justice would have a chance.

At each high point along the trail, he searched in front and in back of him, but he saw no other riders. They may have decided to turn tail and run afterall, he thought. But as he reasoned it out more, he decided the men would be in Prescott. Hart had no place to run to south. He might go north, west or east. Any of them meant Prescott first for supplies. Those two men could never travel on Apache rations.

About eleven o'clock by the sun, Chisholm came to a high point and decided to wait and see if he could spot anyone behind him. He was less than two hours out of Skull Valley, and that was next door to Prescott. He hid the horse in some brush and lay down watching the trail. He had been climbing steadily since leaving Phoenix. The elevation in the little desert community was not quite 1100 feet. In Prescott the elevation would be 5,354 feet. Over a mile in the sky. Gone was the hotness of the valley. The weather was almost crisp now and occasional clouds billowed up like cotton balls on the edge of the hills to his right.

For an hour he lay on the fresh green grass watching the trail. Nothing. Either the murdering pair were ahead of him, or well behind and taking their time.

Back on the trail he urged the black along faster. In a little over an hour he had passed the lonesome ranch at Skull Valley and turned onto the Prescott trail to the east. In the soft ground at the edge of the trail he saw fresh prints. Among them were both the shoe marks he had seen outside the blue and white house in Phoenix — the V and the reinforced U.

Hart and Berger were ahead of him, and by now already into Prescott and, perhaps, through it and out of town. He hurried the black now and made good time.

Prescott was not a booming town in 1872. True it was bigger than Phoenix and large enough to hold the headquarters of the Department of Arizona and the military camp. There were a dozen bars and gambling houses, two hotels that were half way respectable, and enough houses and other business to make up a fair sized frontier town.

He stared in irritation at the saloons. Usually he found them interesting, but now they presented a variety of places where Hart and Berger might be, and he had to find them quickly.

Chisholm got off his black and tied her to

the hitching rail outside the Golden Eagle Saloon. This was as good a place to start as any. He stared down the street guessing how long it would take him to look over each spot. There was no way he could do it quickly. And when he located them, just what in hell would he do next? There was no Apache training that covered a situation like this.

CHAPTER 3
HUP, TWOOP, THREEP, FOUR.

It was a little after four in the afternoon when Wade Chisholm began his rounds of the saloons in Prescott. At the first three he had three warm beers but came up with no sign of the two men. Outside on the boardwalk he took a quick survey of the hitching rails. He wasn't sure what kind of horses the murderers were riding, and it would look a bit strange if he started checking every shod hoof on Main Street.

At the fifth saloon he saw Berger buying a bottle of whiskey from the barkeep. Chisholm watched him and saw him go to a table in the rear of the room where Hart sat with his back to the wall, his hands free at his sides. Hart was ready for any kind of trouble.

As Wade finished his beer he realized the two men must know someone was hunting them. Harry had been snatched, and now the same one would be tracking them. Only they didn't know who the person was. That was Wade's advantage. But here in town he would have to be careful. He had no wish to swing at the end of a gallows rope for dispatching two murderers. Chisholm would bide his time. He picked up another beer and moved over watching one of the poker games in progress, then wandered past a lonely little man playing an out of tune piano. At last he sat down at the table two over from the one occupied by Hart and Berger.

He looked around and for a moment stared directly at Hart. Wade grinned, stood and walked to the table. He toed a chair back and sat down across from them, his back to the door and facing the two.

"Gentlemen, I hope you don't mind if I'm direct?" he said softly. As he talked he inventoried the pair. Hunt was the smaller one, exactly as the rancher's wife had painted him. The inch scar was more prominent than it should have been. His face was thin, almost to gauntness, and there was a bitter hardness about his green eyes. His hat was off now and brown hair was cut short.

"I have a certain operation planned for two days from now, and I need a pair of men who can do two things. One is use a gun and do what they are told. The second is to keep their mouths shut and move on out of town with their share of the profits."

Berger looked at Hunt with a gleam in his eye, but all Hunt did was take a sip of his beer.

"Why us?" Hunt asked, his voice level, unemotional, his green eyes staring hard at Wade.

"Why not? You just got into town, nobody knows you here. I saw you ride in. Neither one of you look like farmers, you're not professional gamblers, and that low-tied hogsleg reminds me of a man I used to know who was almost too good with a six-gun. You sure as hell don't look like hard rock mine rats either."

"We're not miners," Berger said. Hunt looked at him and he kept quiet. Hart had another draw on his beer.

"Say we were interested. How long would this job be?"

"Two days, possibly three. One day to set it up, a short wait, and then the action, the split, and a quick ride out of town."

"I like quick work," Hart said. He was in no rush. He watched a fading blonde try to do a dance on the small stage. She dissolved into giggles, reached for a whiskey someone handed her and jumped into a man's waiting arms.

"If we were interested, what kind of pay are you talking about," Hart asked.

"Enough for everybody. I'm not greedy." Wade took a swallow of his beer now, letting them wait. "I'm not exactly sure how much it will be, and it's a bit of a gamble, but the stakes are high. There might be only ten thousand in the box, and then again there might be thirty thousand in gold. The shipment is supposed to have left Denver heading for the San Francisco mint. Not a regular run, a kind of gold wagon."

"With plenty of protection," Hart said. "Probably a hundred cavalrymen will meet them fifty miles out of town and take them fifty miles on past."

"No way. Old George Crook has too much trouble with the Coyotero Apaches down south to worry about government gold. It's as clean as I can get it. I hear four men: a driver, one guard on top and two inside."

"Be a snap," Berger said looking interested.

Again the hard-eyed man stared Berger down and then glanced back at Chisholm. "We'll sleep on it. We had a hard ride up the trail."

"Where are you staying?" Chisholm asked. There was a moment of silence. "I could have followed you and found out. I want to be out front on everything, agreed?"

The hard green eyes weighed him, and Wade seemed to pass the test. "Arizona Hotel," Hart said.

"I'll see you there for breakfast at 8 tomorrow. I'll have to know by then so I can set it up." He stood, took his beer, wandered down the saloon to another table and sat down away from the two killers.

Later he did follow them, and they went into the Arizona Hotel. A front room over the entrance lighted a short time later and Wade checked the register. The men were using their right names and had registered in room 2B front. The price was fifty cents a night for each.

Wade went outside and watched the room for a while, then settled down across the street on a bench near the hardware store. He wanted to burst into the hotel room and gun down both men and surge away into the night. No one would chase him, and it would be over. Maybe. It was a low percentage gamble, especially since the sheriff's office was just across the street from the hotel. A few minutes later Wade melted into the shadows beside the hardware and stood in the alley, hidden from the street.

He waited.

A half hour later Berger came out of the hotel, walking fast with a purpose. Wade trailed him, and after a block realized that someone else was following him. Chisholm ran forward to catch Berger but before he could get there, two men jumped out from an alley with six shooters drawn. They never said a word, just ushered him ahead to where Berger stood in front of the light coming from the Nugget Saloon.

A tall man with a military bearing went forward and whispered to Berger.

"Why are you following me?" Berger asked Wade.

"Following you? I was trying to catch you. You were almost running, for Christ's sake. I wanted to tell you something more about what we talked about before."

Berger lifted his brows, motioned the other men back, then nodded.

"It could have waited, but when I saw you come out . . . it's just that I've got information. My source in Denver said the big bundle, the heavy box was put on the private stage. It should be going past here in two days. There will be at least $30,000 in the box. Maybe twice that. Now, that is a hell of a lot more than any of us can make in a dozen bank jobs if we hit it good. That's a big mark, and I'll split it three ways."

Berger nodded. "Yeah, sounds good. Only we got a problem."

"Who the hell are these bodyguards of yours? You got yourself a whole tribe of protectors?"

Berger nodded. "Sort of. I can't get into that." He seemed undecided. "Well, we'll talk about it with you at breakfast." Berger turned and walked away. One of the men went with him, the other two had melted back somewhere off Main Street.

Wade turned, hooked his thumbs in his belt and walked up the main stem to his hotel. He'd done everything he could for now. The next order of business was to get some sleep. He probably would be needing it.

At the hotel he decided on a hot tub bath and paid the fifty cents for a boy to bring up five buckets of hot water for the bath tub down the hall. He luxuriated until the water cooled down, then shaved and dropped off to sleep like a new born puppy.

The next morning Wade woke refreshed, and went to the Arizona Hotel shortly before 8 a.m. and waited in the small lobby. Not many were having breakfast.

41

Hart and Berger came in. They nodded, and Wade followed them into the dining room. Hunt had shaved. He picked out a table and sat down first.

Chisholm sat across from him. "What's your decision," Wade asked. "Do you want to make a lot of money fast, or keep on grubbing for it?"

Hunt shot Chisholm an irritated glance, then tapped his fingers on the table as a young girl, the daughter of the hotel owner, hurried up and took their orders. When she left, Hunt looked at Chisholm.

"No, we're not going to be working with you. Too much risk on a government thing. Anyway, we've got something else that has developed, and this one is a sure thing."

"So, that's it," Chisholm said, sounding surprised but sure that they wouldn't go for the plan. "Well, your loss, men. I won't have any trouble finding adequate help. Maybe next time." He rose, moved to another table and asked the waitress to bring his stack of hot cakes and bacon to where he was. Chisholm ate quickly and was out of the hotel before the other two.

Chisholm didn't follow them. He figured they would be leaving town soon and that they had put their horses in the livery. Instead, he waited near the stable.

An hour later the two men arrived, paid for their horse's keep and saddled up. By ten they were on the trail heading for Flagstaff and Wade Chisholm followed them. He wasn't on the trail, rather he worked through the low brush and trees off the trail, keeping the men in sight most of the time.

Five miles out of town in a hilly stretch that moved up and down sharply, Chisholm rode well ahead of the two and picked out a perfect ambush spot. It was a narrow ravine as the trail worked up to a pass. Wade lay in wait behind some rocks with his Spencer and a handful of extra rounds. He waited for an hour and the pair hadn't showed up on the trail. It was the only one headed in this direction. He got his horse and back-tracked the trail until he found where their shoe prints turned off onto a faint trail into the brush. He could see a valley beyond. At the head of the lane was a sign: "Continental Divide Mining Company. Private Property, Keep out."

Chisholm rode a quarter of a mile back toward town, moved the black off the trail into the woods and left his hat with the tied up horse. He ran silently back to the lane and followed it toward the valley, parelleling it as he worked through the woods a hundred feet to one side. He was gliding from one tree to the next when he spotted a guard on the lane, a quarter of a mile in from the road. The man was bored, smoking, standing guard at a makeshift barrier of a counter balanced log across the trail.

Chisholm passed the guard without his knowing it and moved on through the light woods toward the end of the lane where it came out of cover into a half-mile long valley.

Lying under a pine tree and a scattering of brush at the edge of the valley, Chisholm used the binoculars he had picked up in Prescott and scanned the valley. At the far end he saw a ranch house, smoke coming from the chimney, and behind it a half dozen other buildings that looked like they might at one time have been part of a mining operation. They didn't look that way now. There was no heavy machinery in sight, no stamping mill, no rail lines and no tailings of worthless overburden. What tailings there were had been grown over by ten years of grass and brush. He had to get closer.

Staying well under cover in the edge of the brush, he ran at an Apache trot around the edge of the valley. He found no people or activities as he approached the far end.

Without warning he heard a shot ahead. Wade dropped to the ground and didn't move. Slowly his head edged upward until he could see ahead. Nothing. He watched longer and at last saw a head rise over a log thirty yards ahead. The man wore a military cap resembling a confederate soldier's cap from the Civil War.

The man stood now and waved his hand forward in the standard infantryman's signal to advance. To Wade's surprise a dozen men leaped to their feet and hurried forward.

In a moment he saw that they weren't headed toward him. They angled off into the deeper part of the trees and up an incline. The man who was the leader wore chevrons on his sleeves and Chisholm had the feeling it was a military training session. Not a word was spoken. The sergeant gave hand motions and changed the direction of the probe. The squad of men broke into a run, dashing forward through the trees until they were out of sight.

Chisholm rubbed his face in puzzled frustration. What on earth was that? He filed the information and moved on around the fringe of the woods until he was as close as he could come to the buildings. Now he was within 50 yards of the ranch house. The last of the unpainted frame warehouse structures was less than twenty feet from the heavy woods. He worked up as close as he could without being spotted and waited, watched and listened.

Men were drifting around the area, some going in and out of the ranch house and the other buildings. No one seemed to be in a rush. Two men with beards wandered over near his hiding place and began throwing six-inch hunting knives into a big pine tree, then having a contest aiming at a bit of cloth hooked on the rough bark.

"When the hell is this operation anyway?" one of the men asked the other.

"I don't know. They said come, so here I am. Hell, I'm in no rush to go back. This is like it used to be, remember?"

"Sure, parts of it were fine. You remember the good times. It's the blood and the hurt and the dying part you forget."

"Hell, you had it easy, no hard duty for you. You spent all your time in the rear areas. I was with the Tennessee Volunteers, infantry by God! We put in three years of hard duty."

"Sure and you came out a private with a yankee minnie ball in your leg and a case of the shakes."

"And no Yankee pension."

"But Abe gave you your dollar and a mule."

"Sure, and like everybody else I drank up the dollar and killed the damn mule." They both laughed.

"We should have a picture of General Grant for our target," the smaller man said sticking his knife in the tree.

Chisholm pulled back and moved around toward the next building that backed up to the brush. Why was a pair of ex–rebel soldiers here in the mountains outside Prescott, Arizona?

At first no one was near the second building. Then he heard shouted commands, drill commands, and a squad of ten men marched briskly into the cleared area between the buildings and stood stiffly at attention.

A man came from the back of the building, strode smartly to the men, stopped in front of them and barked an order. They snapped into a precise parade rest position, their eyes straight ahead.

"Gentlemen, we are here for a purpose. You have been told it will be a glorious victory for the South, that it will help us hold up our heads again as real men. The war is over and lost, we all realize that, but for some of us there is a higher calling than buckling under to the yankees and black bastards and letting them run our states.

"This is a select company you are in, and you men are the elete squad of the whole group. To you will go the most honors, the most glory, and the greatest risk. You all are volunteers and I salute you. Now, rest well, every man here has the next two days off. Do anything you wish: hunt, fish, utilize barracks C, and eat. Our orders should be coming down soon." The man turned, saluted another man who promptly dismissed the detail in best military fashion.

Chisholm remained hidden in the brush trying to realize if what he had just heard could be true. A gathering of southern rebels in Arizona? And the men, obviously, were militarily well trained and had been here for some time. How many of them were there? What weapons did they have? Would they have cavalry or be all infantrymen? A column of two hundred mounted bluecoats from the U.S. 5th Cavalry would make short work of the rebels if General Crook knew about them. But in the melee the two men Chisholm was most interested in might get away. He couldn't permit that.

Wade moved on around the periphery of brush, checking on the other buildings, trying to determine how many men were in the complex. He saw more marching units, in groups of ten, some much better trained than others, but all showing the precision of old-hand soldiers. This could be a potent force if it were not stopped. He should tell General Crook at once, but he hesitated. Perhaps, he should be a volunteer himself. He didn't know what the routine was to get an invitation, but he could fake the rest of it. The Tennessee Second Volunteers. That was the outfit he'd heard a lot about. They were flashy, devil-may-care units. Yes, he'd go out and brush up on his southern accent and come back dripping magnolia blossoms and you-alls.

At least there was a plan now.

He worked his way out of the area, found his horse untouched, and rode back to town. There was a message for him in the key box at the hotel. He read it twice, but couldn't make any sense of it.

"Mr. Chisholm. I understand you're to be in town only for a short stay, so I must see you at once. I'm leaving Friday. It is urgent that I see you. I'll be in contact." It was signed only with initials J.T. Initials always worried Wade.

He read the paper again, put it in his pocket and went up the hotel steps to his second floor room. He was determined to soak up some southern manners and voice inflections without overdoing it. He was mentally practicing as he climbed the steps and turned the key in his door, or he might have been more prepared. Wade opened the door, went in and closed it. Only then did he see the gun pointing at him. It was an army Colt .44 and the grip was firm and steady. The surprising thing was that a remarkably pretty girl held the gun. She was small, compact with soft blonde hair, a long, elegant neck and a sweet face that was now twisted into a frown.

"Don't move, Mr. Chisholm, just turn around and lean against the wall, then slide down it slowly until you're seated. Then put your hands behind your back and lean on them and cross your legs."

He started to laugh, but saw her finger tightening on the trigger. He knew how easy some of those army .44's could go off.

"I don't want to have to shoot you right now, Mr. Chisholm, but I certainly will if I have to. I'll tear my clothes and tell them you attacked me and that's why I shot you. I'll tell them I really didn't mean to kill you, I was only trying to protect my honor. Now sit down, quickly!"

Wade Chisholm knew people well enough to realize the girl was overwrought and worked up to a pitch that she could do exactly what she said. He slid down the wall, crossed his legs, folded his arms behind him and leaned against them. He was helpless. What in the world was this pretty girl doing here threatening him with a gun?

CHAPTER 4
A SHOOTER TALKING.

"Miss, I'm sorry, but I don't believe I know you."

"You most certainly *do not* know me, Wade Chisholm, but I know you."

"As you can see you have me at an extreme disadvantage. Oh, are you by any chance the J.T. who left a note in my box earlier downstairs?"

"Yes."

"Well, at least now we are making progress. What does the J stand for: Jennie, June, Jenny?"

"No, Jocelyn, not that it matters. We are going to sit and wait for a while, and then later, when it's safe, I'm going to shoot you dead, then slip out of the back of the hotel to my horse and ride back home."

"Oh, then you are from this area. You must be army, that's an army .44 you're waving around. Do you think you put the rounds into the chamber properly? Be a shame if it jammed and wouldn't fire at all." He thought she might make the mistake of looking down to check the weapon. He held his hands pressed hard against the wall ready to push outward toward her legs.

Her stare never wavered. "That kind of trick won't work on me, Mr. Chisholm. And don't worry, I've used this same .44 many times in the last three years. My father taught me to shoot extremely well. Sometimes I beat him."

"At targets."

"What?"

"Targets, you were shooting at targets."

"Naturally, and hitting the bull's eye."

"But Jocelyn, have you ever shot at another human being before, or at anything alive, even a rabbit?"

She stared at him without speaking.

"I didn't think so."

"But now I can. I've never been this furious with anyone before, never."

"So now you're mad and that makes you judge, jury, and the executioner all rolled into one small girl. Don't you think the accused and convicted should be told what dastardly crimes he's dying for?"

"You already know."

"Like who did I kill, your mother? I bet that's it, I killed your mother with a butcher knife, cutting off her head, right?"

"Don't be idiotic, my mother is fine."

As he spoke Wade was trying to think of who he knew in the army at the base here whose last name started with T, and an officer at that. T . . . T . . . T. And then he had it. Thornton. Yes, he remembered that Captain Thornton had a family on the camp site in Prescott. It must be the Thornton girl. Now he understood how she might think she had a case.

"Well, so I do know, let's just say for the sake of argument that I don't. Instead let me tell you a short story. It's about a man who led a patrol into Indian territory and engaged the Chiricahua in a skirmish. Now that's a worthwhile, practical job for an officer to do, right? But when I made contact with this group of Indians, I felt myself exploding into a panic. I threw down my weapons and hid behind a rock screaming and wailing. I failed in my job to order my men in the attack. I let a dozen of my men be killed who shouldn't have been. I failed to give direction, to order my men to take cover and to resist and to move them when and where they needed for a successful conclusion to the battle. I was a coward under fire. A subordinate had to take over and extricate the troop as well as he could, and at the same time try to take out the officer who had turned into a coward under fire."

The girl stared at him, her frown deepening. "I don't know what you're talking about. I'm not going to kill you because you were a coward under fire."

"Then why?"

"You know perfectly well, why. Don't act so innocent."

"All right, let's say that I didn't lead that patrol we just talked about. Let's say I was the second in command and I had to try to save as many of the men as I could as well as save the officer who was the coward under fire. What do you think I should have done after I got back to the post? What should I have said about the officer who failed and showed cowardice?"

"I really don't care, and I don't understand what you're saying, and it won't do you any good to try to talk your way out of this. I'm going to kill you just as soon as it's safe."

"I don't think you are, Jocelyn, and you don't either. Oh, I know you're angry with me, but you realize you haven't heard both sides of the story. Have you?"

"What do you mean, Mr. Chisholm?"

"What we're trying to do is keep your

father alive. We're trying to let Captain Arthur J. Thornton resign his commission before he gets himself and a lot of good cavalrymen slaughtered should he panic again under fire."

Her face went white. "Then it was you! You are one of them. I've been waiting for you to admit it, so I know I don't make a mistake." She lifted the weapon higher aiming at his head, only now the tip of it wavered and her hand shook.

"Jocelyn, your father simply isn't emotionally able to be an army officer any more. Not in the field. Not ever again. He once could and must have been excellent at it. But now he's getting men under him killed. Fourteen men have died who shouldn't have, and it's your father's fault. He should have been court-martialed after Swallow River Camp. Let him go back to Boston and work in the bank and be happy."

Her face twisted in fury. "Last night Daddy tried to kill himself. He slashed both wrists. Luckily, we found him and got the blood stopped. He's still very weak, but alive."

He closed his eyes and sighed. "I'm sorry, I didn't know." Concern flavored his voice. "Has he talked with General Crook yet?"

She nodded. "It was right after that, that he tried. . . ."

"Damn him! Why didn't he accept himself as he is now and simply resign?"

"My father is not a quitter."

Wade had been moving his hands slowly away from his back and had them now lying at his sides as he judged the distance to the girl.

"Don't try it, Mr. Chisholm, I'm more determined than ever."

"Then you're as big a fool as your father is. He simply had too much killing and slaughter, he saw too many men get their heads blown open and their brains spilled out. He saw too many charges that left women and babies dead and dying. Give the man a break. Let him resign with some dignity."

"But you don't understand. Daddy still doesn't *believe* that he did those things. He can't accept it. And he hates the banking business."

"Yes, I can see how he might not like . . ." As he said it Chisholm sprang upward with a push from his hands and both feet, slapped the gun aside and fell against the girl.

As soon as his hand hit the gun and pushed it aside, her finger contracted and the weapon went off. The bullet missed him but the roar of the .44 in the small room was like a thunderous explosion and both of their ears rang from the sound of it.

His leap carried them both backward and they fell on the bed. He lay there a moment, then twisted the gun out of her grasp and stood up.

Someone pounded on the door. He went to the panel and opened it. Six or seven people were in the hall.

"Sorry folks, I was getting ready to clean old Betsy here and I dropped her and the damn thing went off. Nothing hurt. Sorry to disturb any of you." He waved, closed the door and turned the skeleton key in the lock.

"Now, young lady," he said turning back to her and putting the key in his pants pocket. "You and I are going to have a long serious talk."

She sat up, tears crawling down both cheeks.

"Damn!" she said. "I don't seem to be able to do anything right."

Chisholm touched her shoulder and she looked up in surprise at the gentle contact.

"Jocelyn, I think you're a remarkable young lady. Who else would try to kill to protect her father?" He went to the window, looked out, then drew up the straight backed wooden chair and straddled it, leaning against the back with his hands on his chin. "Now, I'll tell you exactly what we're going to do."

She stared angrily at him.

"I suppose you're going to rape me."

Chisholm laughed. "Not even if you wanted me to. What you are going to do is go back to the camp and have a long talk with General Crook. Tell him what has happened, that you talked to me, and that I insisted that you talk with him. George Crook is a general, but he's also one of the most compassionate men I've ever known. He's fair, he's honest, and he's doing what is best for your father. If I can't convince you of that, I'm sure he can.

"After that you're going home and talk to your father every day until he's strong enough to travel. You're going to convince him that he must get out of the west *because of you.* Tell him that you'll go crazy if you have to stay in this Godforsaken place another week. Beg him to take you back to Boston. Tell him that you need him to take care of you. Tell him you don't even care if he quits the army. He should have been a general himself by now, so why doesn't he quit and go back to Boston where they have music and dancing and eligible young men a girl can pick and choose from. Your job is to convince him that you need him to do this *for you,* and *for your mother.* If you give him a purpose for the move, a reason why he must go back, it will be easier for him. Don't once mention the Salt River or Swallow River Camp. Make it easy for him to resign from the army."

He watched her. She had stopped crying and was blinking soft blue eyes. She seemed to be listening to him carefully.

"We do want to go back east, but father still doesn't want to resign."

"Jocelyn, it isn't up to him any more. If he doesn't resign, he will be court-martialed, convicted, disgraced and discharged from the army dishonorably. You don't want that to happen. He has no choice. Just as you have no real choice. Convince him that you and your mother *need* him to take you to Boston, and there should be some aspect of the banking world that he can fit into without much pain. Show him that he's done enough for the army, that now it's time he pays you and your mother some attention."

She stood and paced the small room. He kept talking, repeating the same ideas, the same arguments, but toward the last he wasn't sure if she heard him or not. Then she came to his chair and looked down at him.

"You are right, Mr. Chisholm. I didn't know all sides of the problem when I first came in. I apologize for trying to kill you."

"I forgive you. Especially since you missed."

She grinned, and he saw dimples sink into both cheeks.

"Now let me see if I understand everything that you've told me." She went over his arguments almost word for word, and in the end made an intelligent and impassioned plea for her father to get her and her mother out of this pest hole, this end of the world.

When she finished she leaned down and kissed him on the cheek, then stepped back quickly.

"Now, Mr. Chisholm, I think it's time you let me slip out without anyone seeing me leave. I don't want to get the reputation as a loose woman."

He nodded. "Jocelyn, just how old are you?"

"Guess!" she said, the little girl slipping through delightfully.

"Nineteen?"

61

She rushed up and kissed his cheek again. "Oh, thank you Mr. Chisholm! I wish I were, but that's close. I'm sixteen."

He stood quickly and smiled. "Well, fine. Now I think it's time for you to slip out of the room. Can I see you back to the camp?"

"Oh, goodness no. I will need my revolver back though. I always carry it when I come into town."

He smiled and gave her the weapon which she tucked away in her skirts. He unlocked the door, opened it quietly and nodded. She went into the hall, smiled once more at him and walked away.

Chisholm sighed and locked the door again. He sat on the bed and tried to remember everything he could about the Tennessee Second Volunteers. He couldn't even pick out a single commanding officer's name, not a general. He'd have to slide over that part somehow. No, better, he'd tell them about the wound he had late in the war and now he didn't remember as well as he used to. But he did know soldiering. Suddenly he was hungry. Chisholm washed in the porcelain bowl and combed his hair. More of the brown was coming out to leave it the natural red. He'd stained his hair a brownish black when he went into the Chiricahua country a month ago. All of the color was not out of it yet. He would have to cut it short again, that would take care of some of the problem.

In the little dining room at the hotel, Chisholm ate beef stew and had apple pie for dessert, then returned to his room. He was asleep by a little after eight that evening and didn't hear a thing until six the next morning. He got up refreshed, renewed and ready for a quick breakfast before embarking on a ride into the past, into the rebel land to the north, into the New Rebel Army of Prescott, Arizona.

Later that morning on the ride out of town, Chisholm put together a new name for himself, a new identity. He was now Jim Jefferson from Nashville, Captain Jim Jefferson of the Tennessee Volunteers. If they asked which unit, he'd say the Thirtieth. He thought he remembered that one. Then he'd use his wound bit, and say he hadn't forgotten how to fight. As a fighting man he was one of the best. He'd had a company for much of the war.

Yes, that should do it. His mind ready, he rode faster.

Chisholm stopped at the gate on the trail that led into the mining company. There was a dinner bell there and he rang it several times. Nothing happened. He fired three shots from his six gun and reloaded, rang the bell again and gave a rebel yell.

Suddenly two rifles aimed at him from the sides of the trail and a voice barked out commands.

"Off your horse, keep your hands high. Stand at ease."

Wade complied and turned toward the voice. Another voice came from behind him.

"What the hail are you a doing? This here's private property."

He turned and faced a man wearing blue jeans and a cotton flannel shirt. He was about thirty, lean, tough looking.

Chisholm braced into attention. "Soldier, don't give me any of your mouth. Open this gate and take me to your commanding officer. I'm Captain James Jefferson of the Tennessee Volunteers, and I demand to see whoever's in charge."

"You ready for the booby hatch? This here's a mining company, we dig in the ground. We don't got no commanding officer but we do have a boss who eats nails for breakfast. You sure you got the right place?"

"Damn sure, soldier, and you-all doing a good job. Now, just tell your commander that Captain Jefferson is here. He may have heard of me from the war."

"We ain't hiring no more hands, you better move on."

He saw that the rifles had been removed. In one swift move his hand slid downward and came up with his six gun aimed at the chest of the man now no more than six feet away.

"Tell your friend with the rifle if he even picks it up again, you are one dead Reb." He gave a rebel yell and motioned with the gun. "Now, open them gates, you heah? Or I'll have you-all come with me to see the colonel."

The man under the gun shrugged. "Open it, Clay," he said. "Well, let the nut through. Go on in, make an ass of yourself. Hit don't bother me no nevermind. You'll come yappin' out minus some teeth, probably, or maybe with one of your own slugs in your hide."

"Soldier, that's fine, you played your part well." Wade stepped into the saddle still keeping the man under his gun. A second man opened the counter-balanced gate, and Wade rode through. He put the gun away and rode slowly now, but in the middle of the trail. There should be another guard soon.

The challenge came from a man behind a

tree and the rifle was aimed at him.

"Hold it right there. Who the hell are you?"

"Captain Jim Jefferson, Tennessee Volunteers, reporting for duty. Where can I find your commanding officer?"

"Another one. Hell, man. This is a mine operation. If you don't have the right words, you don't get in here. You should know that."

"Young man, come here!" It was a command.

"Aw, shit! What you think you're doing. Go back where you came from."

"Soldier, get out here this instant!"

The man stepped out, the rifle still trained on Wade. He wore the semi-military uniform, but not really military. Somewhere between that and a standardized worker's factory suit.

"Now, I'll tell you again, young man. I don't know what the problem is. I'm Captain James Jefferson of the Tennessee Volunteers, and I demand to be taken to your commanding officer."

"You demand just anything you want to. . . ."

"Soldier, point that weapon away from me or you're dead. I'm going to draw my revolver and fire six times in the air. That should get someone here with some authority." Wade watched the rifle muzzle lower as he drew slowly. He fired into the air, emptying his weapon. He calmly reloaded the revolver and before he was done, a pair of horses pounded up to the point where he sat. The riders both had on the same paramilitary type uniform. One had a rebel cap on.

Wade calmly put his weapon back in the holster and looked at the two men.

"I can't tell if either of you are officers, but if you are, my name is Captain James Jedediah Jefferson, lately of Nashville, and formerly with the Tennessee Volunteers. I am demanding to see your commanding officer and these stupid enlisted men don't seem to understand."

The older of the two men smiled. He was about 35 and wore the rebel cap.

"Captain, sir. I don't think you understand. This is a mining company. We had let it be known that we were operating and looking for some southern workers who might want to help us get the mine going. That's the end of it. We don't need any more help, and we're set for some time to come."

"Yes, remarkable. Good security. Top notch. I commend you. But as you know this is the time in history when the South must rise to an occasion. This is one time we can strike a blow for the South that will be forever remembered and after which we can return to our homes and jobs and businesses and at least be able to hold up our heads a little higher, and not vomit when them Damn Yankees and the Black Bastards run all over us with impunity!"

He watched his words take effect on the two riders. He was sure they had heard them before or something much like them. Wade charged on.

"The orders should be coming down any day now, sir. And I want to be part of the fight. I don't know what it is, but I'll be glad to take a demotion to Second Lieutenant for a berth. I'll even take a platoon instead of a company. Now, without any more of this security charade, I'd like to see the colonel."

The men on the horses looked at one another, and then abruptly the older one drew his revolver and held it aimed at Wade as he rode slowly toward him.

"Sir, I'm sorry, but I'll have to place you under arrest. You are now our prisoner and as an officer and a gentleman I'll have to ask you to hand over your weapon. You are on private property and it is our right to restrict movement on this land. Your weapon, sir, if you please?"

CHAPTER 5
THE OLD REBEL YELL

"And if I chose not to give it to you, sir?"

"Then things could get downright unpleasant, sir. Give me your weapon and we'll arrange a meeting down the trail with one of the mining officials. He can tell you anything you want to know about our company."

"Is he the colonel?"

"I'm afraid you'll have to wait and see who from the company comes to talk to you."

Wade shrugged, lifted his .44 from the holster by a thumb and finger so there could be no mistake, then took it by the barrel and handed it to the other man.

"Thank you, sir. Now, if you'll follow me, we'll go see what this is all about."

Wade rode behind the first man and saw the other one come in behind him and take out his revolver. In effect, he was a prisoner, but at least he would find out what was going on. Wade doubted that they would go anywhere near the Ranch House. He was right.

A half mile down the wooded trail they had not yet come to the valley. Instead, they had been winding around the near end of it. They came to a small log cabin that was at least 30 years old. It was in good condition, chinked and even had a trail of blue smoke coming from a rock and mortar chimney.

Wade was instructed to dismount, then the older man led him into the building. It had a dirt floor packed hard, one window without glass and a burning kerosene lamp. Behind a rough hewn table sat a man in his fifties with steel-gray hair, a thin face and eye glasses featuring piercing eyes. His whole body seemed to be slender, hard, active. He glanced up in irritation when they came through the door.

"We have another one, sir," the guard said.

"Sir, Colonel, sir. I'm so glad I found you. These trashy people keep treating me like nobody. I'm Captain James Jefferson, formerly with the Tennessee Volunteers, Infantry, and reporting for duty, sir. I'd be happy to take a reduction in rank, sir, just so I can be involved. I want to *do* something. I know you understand, suh. I know your final orders have not come down yet, but that they should be here shortly. God, man. I would even take a platoon to get in on something exciting, something that could let some of us Southerners hold up our heads again."

The slender man stared at him. "What the hell are you talking about?"

"Come, now, Colonel. I think the game is well played out. I'm here to work, to serve. I'll train, lead. Just give me a position, a command."

"You say you were with the Tennessee regiments? Which one?

Wade rubbed his head. "The Second . . . I think, sir. I did get a wound to the head the last month, and now I don't remember that part too well, sir. They say I should have died, but as you can see, I didn't. I'd be glad to take any command sir." His accent wasn't perfect, but he was putting just a slight touch into it, as if he'd lived away from the south for a while.

"I asked about which Tennessee group because I was with the Volunteers, too." His eyes closed for a moment. "I'm sorry, I wish we had a place for you, but our mining operation is just getting started. Perhaps later you might stop back and ask the guard at the gate. I wouldn't think there would be anything for at least six months. Maybe come spring."

"All right, whoever you are! Enough of the bullshit! I came here to see the colonel. I *demand* to see the colonel. I know what's going on here, the raid, the orders coming down, all the soldiers. I want to be in on it. You have a choice, sir. Either you take me to the colonel, or when you rush me back out onto the trail, I'll go straight to General Crook at Prescott and he'll come boiling in here with 400 Cavalrymen and blow your little outpost of rebels to hell!"

The thin man behind the desk stood. "My name is Brown, Lawson Brown. We have to be very careful here, Captain. All I can do is pass you to the next clearance and see what they say. However I think I should warn you that they have the option of dealing with situations like this with extreme prejudice. If they think you're lying or that you present any kind of threat such as you just suggested to me, they will kill you on the spot before you can get your mouth open to protest. Just a friendly reminder. We may appear to be a bit slovenly, but that promotes our mining company image, don't you see."

"I'm not used to being threatened. . . ."

"You are in no position to make threats

yourself, Captain, or to suggest methods or procedures. If you don't like the way you're handled here, there are other methods." The small man's black eyes glinted dangerously.

"I'm a soldier, sir. I follow orders."

"Good. These men will take you to the next stop." The thin man went back to the papers on his desk, dismissing Chisholm without even a glance or a wave.

"This way, sir," one of the two riders said as he approached the door. "We have a short ride ahead."

The three men mounted and again the order was the same, with Chisholm between them. They rode around the outside of the valley on a well worn trail, and only when he sensed they were near the valley on the far side, did they stop.

"I'm sorry, sir, we'll have to blindfold you now. Orders, and we always follow orders."

"Yes, of course. Carry on."

They put a bandanna around his eyes and tied it securely behind his head, then rode again. The man in front led his horse. He felt a light breeze on his face and the warmth of the sun on his cheek, and he realized they were out into the sun. No more than five minutes of slow riding and they stopped. He was helped down.

Inside a building, he walked along what

he guessed was a hall, then into a room with carpet on the floor. He heard a door shut and lock. The blindfold was removed and he found himself in an office with a rich mahogany desk in front of him. A large window opened onto the woods and a peak in the distance.

Looking out the window was a large man with handlebar moustache and long sideburns but no chin whiskers. He was massively built, broad shoulders, thick arms and a huge chest. He wore the same simple blue uniform the rest of his men wore.

"You don't look like a miner," the big man said.

"Please, Colonel. No more of this idiocy about a mining camp. I am here to help the South, do what I can for her even at this late and lamented time. And, Suh, that is the only reason I am here."

The large man went to the desk, sat down and looked at a piece of paper. "You call yourself a captain from the Tennessee Second Volunteers. I don't believe that for a minute. What I do believe is that you know far too much to be turned loose. You made a threat that could quickly get you killed. Worse, you give the impression that you know more than you should."

The big man left his desk and walked in

front of Wade whose own 6-1 felt small as he looked up at the 6-4 man. Without a word, the stranger's ham-like fist powered toward Wade's belly. He saw it coming only at the last moment and surged backward to lessen the impact, but still he was dropped to the floor by the force of it and rolled over gasping for breath.

As Wade tried to sit up he heard the same rich voice go on with the particulars.

"You're right, Jefferson. We're not a mining company, and we are damn particular about who we let in here. You simply rode in off the trail, without a password, without any of the required signs or countersigns. You never were recruited by our people, and if you were, you're a month too late. We think you're a plant, not from the army, or the government. Maybe just from the town to try to find out what we're doing. You know too much to be unimportant.

"It takes a lot of food to feed all these men, and certain questions have been raised in Prescott. But a few yankee dollars quieted most of them. Until now. Get up!"

Wade faked his inability to rise and strong hands grabbed him from behind and lifted him, then spun him against the wall. His pockets were turned inside out, and he was searched carefully.

He had no papers on him with any name, nothing to connect him with the army or his right name. Not even a letter with an address on it. The searchers were disappointed.

"No identification at all is worse than a fake set, Mr. Jefferson, or whatever your name might be. You've got five seconds to tell me who you are and why you're here."

"Captain James Jefferson, Second Tennessee, First Regiment, A Company."

The fist powered into him again and he lashed out, without trying to hurt the man, but knowing he should put up some defense.

"I know who you're trying to kill. All I want to do is help!" Wade cried in pain and frustration. The fist came at him again, this time aimed for his jaw and he felt it hit and jolt him. His eyes refused to focus and he realized he was falling. He hit the floor and rolled over, the silky folds of darkness draped over his mind.

When he woke up he was lying on a wooden floor, in another room. The boards over the windows were bar like, letting light in. It was still daylight. He touched his jaw and winced. The man's fist was like a sledgehammer. He was a prisoner. That meant he hadn't fooled them, but he had confused them enough so they didn't shoot him outright. They were worried.

If they asked, he would tell them about his backup of 40 cavalrymen and his hourly report schedule and all sorts of ingenious plans to get information out of the valley to his friends. If they asked. On the other hand, if they opened the door and used a double barreled shotgun, he wouldn't have time to do anything but die.

He sat up and found that his body still functioned. The knockout punch to his jaw had saved him any real damage. Chisholm's head spun for a few seconds after he sat up, then cleared. Slowly he got to his feet, swaying a little until his balance resumed. Wade walked quietly to the window and checked it. The inch-thick boards were held in place by nails, three inches long, at least by the size of the nail heads. The door might be another matter. Wade tried the knob, knowing it would be locked. But the lock was the primitive type. Quickly he unlaced his right boot. He wore army officer type boots and utilized them as hiding places for several small tools. One of those was a stiff piece of wire which he took out, then laced up the boot. He fashioned the wire into a simple twist key-type probe. The "skeleton" key locks were simple to open. With the wire bent into the proper shape, he twisted it with the leverage of the long handle. With great satisfaction he heard the slight metallic click as the lock opened. He could see through the keyhole but there was nothing but a wall across a hall.

Gently he pushed the wire back into his boottop, then turned the knob and opened the door a quarter of an inch. He saw only a sliver of the hallway. No one seemed to be there. No guard. He opened it a little more, then heard a door open down the hall. He slid the panel closed, letting the knob turn as the door latched.

Footsteps and voices sounded outside as two or three men came toward him. He heard a few words of the conversation, but could make no sense of them. When the steps faded, he repeated the process and looked again. He could see down the hallway to his right. There was a door some 30 feet away. In a sudden move he opened the door far enough so he could look to the left. An outside door showed less than ten feet away. He tensed, watched both ways, then stepped into the hall, closed and latched the door and walked down the hall toward the nearest door as if he belonged there. No one appeared. He stepped through the outside door and found himself near one of the large buildings he had seen from the brush. Chisholm walked as casually as he could toward the woods.

He saw two men pitching horse shoes in the area near the next building. They ignored him. He stepped into the brush as nonchalantly as he could and soon was out of sight.

The plan had been building as he strolled toward safety. Now it came full blown. He needed one of those blue suits. The two men played another round of horse shoes, going from one end to the other. Two ringers at the far end ended the game and one man swore roundly.

"I'm gonna practice until I can get at least one ringer," he said. He threw the shoes at the stake nearest the woods. The other man picked up some money off a rock and laughed, then went into the building.

When the man threw the shoes near the far end next to the woods, Wade had moved to the fringe of the trees and waited. As the man walked up to pick up the shoes, Wade darted out. He caught the man around the throat with his arm and dragged him into the brush. Inside the concealment, Wade stopped, breathing heavily. He had an arm twisted behind the man's back. He pulled him to his feet and walked him a hundred yards into the trees and up a low hill.

Five minutes later the horse shoe thrower was safely tied hand and foot and gagged. Wade put on the newly acquired blue pants and shirt, pushed his red hair under the blue cap, and wandered back to the horse shoe pit. He threw the shoes toward the far stake, then wandered into the next building. It had been set up as a barracks. His practiced eye told him that these were not new men; they had been there for some time.

On the large field between the buildings and the Ranch house, he saw four groups of men taking close order drill. There were ten men in each group. If Horst Berger were in one of the squads he would be easy to spot.

Wade sat down in the shade of a tree where another blue-clad man loafed.

"Howdy," the rebel said.

"Yeah, howdy," Chisholm said. He had surveyed the two squads he had seen so far and knew Horst was not one of the men. No one was as tall as Berger. The third squad came head on for the tree, trotting at double time, then broke to the right not fifteen feet away. Horst Berger led the right hand line in front. Shipley Hart brought up the rear. The blue cap covered Wade's red hair and he moved one hand over his face

81

to prevent either man from recognizing him as they passed.

"Think that bunch will make it?" Wade asked the other man.

"Hail, I don't know. Don't much give a damn. Long as I get the paycheck. You heard anything about when?"

"Yep, coming up, they say. Shortly now, shortly, whatever the hell that means."

The other man stood. "Well, got to get gittin'."

"Yeah," Chisholm said. "Y'all take care." Wade watched the squad of men train for an hour before they were marched to the closest of the large buildings and dismissed. Ten men vanished inside. The new recruit's barracks, Wade decided. He hadn't been in that one.

He wondered how much more time he had? They would discover he was gone before long. And he had no weapons, not even a pocket knife, only his two hands. He frowned. That was how Hannah died, with bare hands, not a weapon. It might be fitting at that.

Wade wandered over to the barracks. He couldn't send in a message. He wasn't sure what names Berger and Hart were using. The killers might be using any name. He had to take the chance and go in after them right now. He used the side door.

Inside the barracks the place looked much like the other, with ten bunks along one wall. The rest of the big building was open and mostly unused. Six men had collapsed on cots. Berger and Hart were not among them. Then at the far end he saw Berger go through a door. Wade walked toward it, wondering when the alarm would sound, wondering when someone would yell at him. But no one did. His shoulders hunched slightly in anticipation of getting a chance at Berger. He was big but didn't look that smart.

There was no sign on the door. He turned the knob slowly, silently, opened the door and looked in.

Berger was pulling a shirt off over his head. No one else was in the room. A bayonet lay on a bunk near the door. Wade picked up the long knife and locked the door behind him.

Wade tapped Berger on the shoulder with the blade.

"Is your name Horst Berger? If it is, I've come here to kill you."

CHAPTER 6
COLD STEEL
BLOODED

Horst Berger clawed the shirt off his face and stared at Wade.

"The hustler from Prescott. Never did think you had a real job for us. I knew you was trouble."

"You couldn't even guess how much trouble, Berger."

"Why?"

"Hannah Miller."

"Who?" Berger seemed genuinely surprised by the name.

"Hannah Miller, you bastard! You killed her and you don't even remember her name. It won't be fast for you. You're going to suffer for as long as possible."

"Hannah Miller? Who's she?"

"The girl in Phoenix you strangled. Have there been that many?"

He understood then. "Back on the trail. You was the one got Harry Carlyle?"

"Yes, the first payment. You're the second."

"I could yell, have ten guys in here in a minute."

"Yeah, but you won't. You think you can take me, even with my blade, right? You're a big man, nobody has ever beaten you, and you know you can put me down and stomp me to death. So come on. Just remember, I'm half Chiricahua Apache. I know more ways to torture a man to death than you've ever thought of. And I'm going to use them all on you."

Berger sprang four feet across the room to a small dresser where he grabbed a six-inch Bowie knife, then grinned and faced Chisholm.

"Come on Breed. You half animal bastard! Come taste my cold steel."

Chisholm held the fourteen inch bayonet like a knife. It was more a cutting tool than for stabbing and looked sharp. He moved to his left, saw the big man shift his weight in readiness to move. Chisholm darted to the right, countered the move and went left as he slashed out with the blade, not really intending to draw blood. Berger jolted backward, realizing he had been outmaneuvered.

"You never fought with a knife before with

anybody but women, have you, woman killer. It's a damn painful way to die."

"You'll be doing the dying, halfbreed."

In the confined space the big man had the advantage, since there wasn't room to dart around, spin, drop, to use the ground, to use all the knife fighting tactics of the Apache. Chisholm began a slow series of thrusts, a herding action, designed to press Berger into the corner.

Berger saw the threat but couldn't prevent it without taking a cut. No blood had been drawn yet. Suddenly Berger bolted from the trap, surged past Wade, and took a heavy slice on his upper left arm he had thrown upward to meet the bayonet. The four-inch long gash spurted blood. Berger looked at it and roared in fury. He held the Bowie by the handle with the point forward. His eyes were twin black holes of hatred as he advanced on Wade.

Wade kept making short thrusts directly at Berger's body, forcing him to dance backwards, to step away with the deadly point only inches from his bare torso.

Berger picked up a straight backed wooden chair and, holding it out to ward off the blade, charged.

Instead of tangling the long bayonet with the chair, Chisholm spun out of the way and jumped as he turned, throwing his booted foot high in a spinning backkick. The surprise move caught Berger off balance, his quarry missing, and the flying hard heel of the boot slammed into Berger's neck. It knocked him down, the knife skittering away from his hand.

As the man's hand reached for the fallen knife, Chisholm stabbed the bayonet downward, the sharp point spearing through the back of Berger's outstretched hand, nailing it to the wooden floor.

Berger screamed, his voice choked off.

Someone knocked on Berger's door.

Chisholm grabbed the Bowie, poised it at Berger's undefended throat and shook his head.

"Berger? What the hell's going on in there?" The voice outside the door demanded an answer.

"Tell him you fell down, and you don't need a wet nurse," Chisholm whispered, forcing the blade to break the skin on Berger's throat.

"Damnit, I fell down, Hart. I don't need you to wet nurse me. Now go away and leave me alone."

"Okay, okay, just quiet it down," Hart said, and a moment later they heard steps going away from the door.

"Don't move, Berger, or I'll slit your throat, then cut off your fingers one by one. Where's your six-gun?"

Berger pointed to the dresser drawer. Wade moved quickly and got the weapon, fastened the belt around his waist and checked the revolver. It had full loads and there were about 30 rounds in the belt.

Chisholm knelt beside Berger. "Now, killer. I'm asking the questions. If you don't answer I start chopping off a finger at a time. If you answer slow, it's another finger gone. Do you understand me?"

Berger nodded.

"Keep it quiet. Now, what is this place all about? Who is the target for the big hit?"

"I . . . I'm not sure. They didn't tell us yet."

The Bowie sliced a shallow blood line on Berger's little finger.

"But you know, you can guess?"

"Some government official. Somebody coming to Denver, and we're going to meet him there. I don't know who."

"How many men are there here?"

"About a hundred and fifty. God, take that blade out of my hand. I think I'm going to pass out."

"Berger, you faint now and when you wake up, you'll be dead. Remember that. Is

88

there a back door out of here to the woods?"

"Yeah."

"How far to the woods from the door?"

"Twenty feet, maybe less."

Chisholm slid the knife into his boot top, stood and with one heave, pulled the bayonet out of the floor and out of Berger's hand. Blood gushed. Chisholm threw Berger a civilian shirt to wrap up his hand. Then he gave him the blue uniform shirt Berger had taken off.

"Put that on, we're going for a hike."

Berger hesitated.

"Any false move, Berger, and the Bowie goes six inches into your gut and twists around, slicing you into mincemeat. You savvy?"

Berger nodded, slid the shirt on and buttoned it.

"If anybody asks, we're slipping out for some target practice. Remember the Bowie will be an inch from your hide."

They saw no one as they opened the door and walked the full length to the back door. Once outside they strolled into the woods without any problems.

When the underbrush covered them, they moved faster until they were two-hundred yards away from the buildings. Chisholm slammed the handgun down on the side of

Berger's head, knocking him to the ground and dropping him into unconsciousness.

When the big man revived, he found himself spread eagled on the ground. His legs were pushed apart and staked down. His left hand was pinned to the ground, but his right hand was held aloft by a stick and his elbow tied down.

Near his immobile right hand burned a small fire. It was the smokeless kind with only extremely dry, dead wood used. The heat that came from the fire was intense, yet the flames never came more than three inches off the ground.

Seated on the other side of the flames was Chisholm.

"Well, our little lad has awakened. Good, the fun and games are about to begin." With a stick, Chisholm pushed the burning wood directly under Berger's flat palm, the same palm caked with blood where the bayonet had slashed through it.

The fire died down as he moved it, but slowly the heat increased and the small finger-sized sticks blazed up again.

Berger exploded in pain and frustration.

"What the hell you trying to do, Injun? You torturing me just for practice?"

"Yes, if that's what you want to believe. Now, how many civilians have you killed in the past seven years?"

"How many. . . . Hell, I don't know. Been riding with Hart. We're Hart's Raiders. Did you know that? Not many people know who we are even. We've been going a lot longer than Cantrell and his bunch ever thought of. How many? Twenty, maybe thirty. I don't know. We're soldiers."

"You're killers. And you strangled Hannah Miller?"

"Yeah, now move the damned fire. Christ, my hand is burning!" He tugged at the stakes but couldn't move his hand away.

"Right, Berger. And by the time the flesh is charred and burned and flakes away, you'll think you're going out of your mind. Then when the first finger burns off you'll probably faint, but I'll bring you back so you can watch the other fingers burn and fall off. By then you'll tell me everything you know."

"Jesus! I already have. I can't take any more of this. I'm ready to pass out again."

"Go ahead, I'll bring you back." Chisholm put two more finger-sized sticks on the fire.

"What is your real name?"

"Horst Berger."

"What is Hart's real name?"

"Shipley Hart. Now kill the damned fire!"

91

"How many men and women had Hart killed in the past seven years?"

"Hart? Maybe two, three. Not many. He always left that to me."

"And you enjoyed it, didn't you, Berger?"

"Enjoyed? Hell, made me feel good. Power. It was up to me! I could let them live or kill them. That's power."

"Like the power I have over you right now, Berger?" Wade stood, knowing that he shouldn't. He stomped out the small fire, then cut the strips of Berger's shirt that had held him tied to the stakes.

"Get up, killer," Wade said. He knew he was making a mistake, going soft. A Chiricahua would never do this. He couldn't torture Berger anymore. His basic Chiricahua instincts had been too dulled and diluted by civilization.

Wade tossed Berger the Bowie knife and picked up the bayonet. This one had a good handle so he could grip it like a fighting knife.

"You have your chance, Berger. You go through me, stomp over my dead body, and you're free."

Berger lunged. It was over almost before it started. Wade side-stepped the bullish charge, thrust the bayonet into Berger's side and saw the blade slant into his body just below the rib cage and drive in full length slanting upward. The blade must have cut the aorta or pierced his heart because Berger stumbled and fell, rolled over and tried to sit up. He lifted the Bowie to throw it, but the lines of communication were down. He dropped the knife, his eyes rolled to one side and he screamed, blowing bubbles of bloody froth from his mouth. His head lolled to one side and his bladder voided at the same time the last gush of air came from his dead lungs.

Chisholm looked at Berger as he might a dead animal.

"That's number two for you, Hannah," he said softly. After wiping the blood off the Bowie on the dead man's pants, Chisholm pushed it into his boot top between flesh and sock, adjusted the gun belt and hefted the .44. It was lighter than he liked but it would shoot, he was sure of that. There was very little that could go wrong with a revolver.

He looked at the body. It should be hidden. He would be missed, but probably not before Chisholm himself was discovered out of his jail room. He gathered leaves, brush and pine needle mulch and covered Berger. Then he normalized the area as well as he could and walked back toward the buildings.

As soon as he stepped into the cleared area, he knew something had happened. Men were rushing around everywhere. A man ran past and he asked him what the trouble was.

"Big trouble. Some bastard slipped inside the camp, and he's loose. We're falling in to count off and then find him. You better get back to your unit." The man ran on.

Wade turned and strolled back into the brush. He had left the .44 and gunbelt on a tree a short ways into the thicket. None of the other men had side arms and it would make him stand out. Now was no time to be unarmed. He wondered if he should go get his civilian clothes. No, he would be too easy to spot. He blended in much better in the blue uniform. He would simply stay low in the brush, wait and see what happened. They couldn't search the entire surrounding mountains for him, and if they tried he could easily stay ahead of them or lose them. He checked the sun. It was about four in the afternoon. The man he had tied up and taken his uniform should have figured out his bindings by now. Wade had made them so the man could get free if he tried hard enough. He wouldn't starve that way.

Chisholm had hidden his own clothes in a tree where the man wouldn't find them. Wade figured he'd want to change back into his regular clothes.

A unit of ten men marched up to the building just ahead of him. One ran to each side and back doors, the rest went in through the main entrance. A moment later the men from inside were marched out, counted, inspected and reviewed. There were ten men in a double column. The inspectors seemed satisfied, dismissed the men and went on to the next barracks. Soon they would find one building with a man short. That would be Berger's group.

Now it would be harder than ever to get Shipley Hart. The man was within a group of 150 armed men who were probably trigger happy now, and all of them were searching for Chisholm. Wait and watch, that was all he could do. As he lay there he heard horses, and from his left two horsemen rode along the trail that circled the valley. They were not searching, just moving from one point to another.

After they passed, Chisholm rose and ran through the brush and timber around the edge of the valley until he could see the barracks where Hart was bunking. It would be the best spot to watch. He was in time to see the inspection team arrive. When the troops fell out there was general confusion, then the words floated to him clearly.

"We're one man short, sir. A man named Berger. Horst Berger. There is blood in his room."

Another man called for attention and the man in charge of the inspection said they would investigate. The nine remaining men were sent to the parade ground for instructions.

The inspection team went inside the barracks, and soon came out. Chisholm had spotted Hart behind the barracks men, apparently he was some kind of noncommissioned officer. If only he had a rifle. He would not hesitate to shoot Hart from ambush. The man was a mad dog and should be terminated. Tonight would have to be midnight requisition time. He needed a rifle and fifty rounds, a good horse and saddle, and a blanket roll.

At the thought of a blanket he smiled. He could just see old Najaha laughing at him for thinking of a blanket. A Chiricahua did not need a blanket. Chisholm grinned. In honor of Najaha, perhaps he would take only half a blanket.

Chisholm watched to the front but saw nothing else happening. He was day dream-

96

ing, not paying enough attention to his problem, or they never would have come up on him that way. For now when Chisholm heard something behind him and turned, it was too late. He found two frowning rebels standing five feet from where he lay. They had worked up in back of him. Slowly he sat up, then stood.

"Welcome," he said in Chiricahua dialect, throwing in the Spanish as well. Then he switched to English. "Welcome, I am Quick Eye, a Chiricahua. Your chiefs have brought me here to help train you."

The men looked at each other in surprise, then one of them lifted the revolver he held and fired.

CHAPTER 7
KNOCK HEADS
REQUISITION

The round blasted past his face so close he could feel the wind. He remained perfectly still, staring at the man who had fired. Chisholm stared hard until the man fidgeted.

"Soldier, that's just cause for me to kill you on the spot, do you realize that? What's your name and unit?" There was a snap, an authority, a military "officer" tone to his voice that brought the two troopers up short. The one who fired holstered his weapon and strained at attention.

"Name, sir. I'm Roscoe Turner, Fourth Unit, sir. Sapper."

Chisholm nodded and looked at the other man.

"Jackson, sir. Henry Jackson, Fourth unit, Sharpshooter."

"I don't know, I don't know," Chisholm said pacing in front of them. "I train you and train you, and then on the first little practice alert, everyone goes crazy. I wanted *veterans.* Men who knew how to function, how to control themselves. I throw a little fake Indian language at you and you know only to shoot first. What's your alert station?"

"The woods sir along the perimeter from barracks one to four. We saw you here, watching the camp. You were acting suspicious. . . ."

"That's enough Turner. Continue your surveillance. I won't report this breech. But keep your finger off the God-damned trigger. Now move!"

Chisholm watched them go out of sight into the brush, took off his big belt and holster, put the .44 inside his shirt and hid the gun belt under some leaves. Then he walked back into camp. It would be safer in there for a while than in the woods, and maybe he could find Hart.

He prowled the camp for an hour, until dusk, and saw only a few units. Hart was with none of them. With darkness he heard details come back into camp. It was his signal to get out. He had no reason to use the gun. In his wanderings he had located the mess hall and got in a short line where sandwiches were being given out. He took four, ate them slowly, not even wanting to know what the filling was. He had a cup of coffee at the end of the line and surveyed the kitchen area. He might need to come back there later that evening.

In the brush he slept until midnight. Some inner alarm warned him of the time and he roused, checked the big dipper circling the North Star and knew it was close to the middle of the night.

His first stop was the mess hall where he found one guard who turned at the wrong time and caught a pistol barrel along the side of the head. Wade took three pounds of beef jerky, two fresh loaves of bread and six apples in a small pack he had rescued. The first barracks he came to revealed rifles stacked in the middle of the room. He took one without collapsing the stack, found a ration of live rounds in a trooper foot locker, and vanished out the door without any of the ten men waking.

Wade vanished into the woods with his loot and carried it to a small knoll overlooking the camp. He stored the pack and the rifle in a hollow oak, then left at an Indian jog toward the stables.

With the horses it was harder. Inbreeding and Apache training gave him an advantage in horse stealing. He knew where the two guards were before five minutes had passed as he lay on his stomach near a small stream and watched the pole corral. One of the guards was by the gate. There were about twenty horses in this corral. He had no idea where the others were, perhaps in a pasture to the north or up some canyon.

The guard at the gate would be the hard one. He decided to take the insider's role. He walked to the corral. When he was within whispering range, he called in a loud stage whisper.

"Hey, don't shoot, it's me, I'm coming around." It worked.

The guard waved and Wade walked around, returned the wave, then slammed his fist into the side of the man's neck twice, putting him on the ground, unconscious. He took his time selecting the horse, wanting a good one with a broad chest for staying power. He wasn't interested in speed. They were quarter horses with some mixes, but he found the one he wanted. In the pale moonlight, he saddled it with a saddle from the top rail and led it to the gate.

The gate creaked as he swung it open. It brought a call from the other guard at a small building thirty yards away.

"Charlie, what the hell's going on down there?"

"Nothing, so keep quiet," Chisholm called

back. He was mounted and at the back of the pack of horses with the gate opened. He gave a piercing Chiricahua scream. The horses perked their ears and one reared. Again Wade screamed, slapped flanks, and waved his hands urging the horses out the gate.

A moment later the twenty head were thundering out the gate and down the valley toward the south. He rode with them, riding low in the saddle. When he was half a mile away from the corral, he swung into the hills and rode a mile behind the knoll where his goods were stashed. In a little meadow he ground-tied the horse so it would have plenty of grazing, then hiked back to his camp and curled up for a few hours sleep. The next day was going to be an interesting one.

He was up with the sun, ate a mouthful of beef jerky and a wide chunk of the brown bread and drank from a nearby spring.

From the edge of the knoll he could see the whole valley and most of the buildings. There was activity all over the area. To the south he saw three squads of men spread out and march through the brush and trees. Across the valley nearer the road two more squads worked through the trees and brush in a search mission.

There could be ten other units out, 150 men. He would have to move cautiously. His first job that morning was to get back in his own clothes. He was through with the uniform. It would be too dangerous to work inside the grounds now. He had another hope in the back of his mind, and now when he moved down toward the tree where he had hidden his civilian clothes, he took the rifle with him. It was a Spencer repeater. He had shot one many times before.

It took him almost an hour to cover the half mile to the tree where he had hidden his clothes. It was a matter of moving to a safe position, then quietly and slowly surveying all the ground he could see for any rebel patrol coming his way. He worked silently, smoothly, got to the tree and changed clothes. Using the same movement technique, he worked his way down where he could see the new recruits' barracks. His brown pants and brown shirt blended into the brown and green of the hills and trees. He built himself a small camouflaged observation point. Entirely covered with limbs and leaves in a stand of brush, he could see the barracks plainly, and by moving two feet forward would have a perfect field of fire toward the barracks. His fervent hope was that Hart would come swinging in with a unit, have to stand at attention for a few seconds so he could sight in on him and blow him half way back to the barracks.

He heard voices and saw a search party coming toward him. They were in a column of twos hiking down the horse trail on their way to a more distant search area. Hart wasn't among the men.

He settled down to wait. Often he had waited as a child at a watering hole or near a game trail for hours without moving, knowing he was downwind and hoping that a deer or a fox would come along. The training proved beneficial.

Chisholm stayed in his blind until nearly four that afternoon when the recruit detail returned from a search. They were tired and dirty. They stood at attention no more than thirty yards away, but each time Wade got Hart in his sights, he moved or the man in front leaned and weaved into the sight and Wade couldn't fire. As they were breaking up the formation he had one chance. He fired, jerked down on the trigger guard, extracted the old shell and pushed a new one into the chamber. His second shot might have grazed Hart's shoulder but Wade wasn't sure. Then Hart was inside the barracks, whistles were blowing and men came running.

Chisholm picked up the empty shell casing and walked back into the woods expecting a chase but wasn't concerned. He would let them see him once, then vanish almost before their eyes. It would be child's play. He had played the game of hunter and rabbit for days on end with the older Chiricahua boys. As it turned out the searchers came no where close to him. He actually sat on a log once waiting for them, but they showed little skill or enthusiasm for the chase, and even less because they knew the rabbit in this case had a repeating rifle.

When the chase was over, Wade returned to the woods near the recruits' barracks. He wondered how Mr. Hart's nerves were about this time. Would the man desert the rebel cause, knowing full well that someone was out there trying to kill him? He had seen two of his Hart's raiders vanish and never seen again, dead perhaps. And now two rifle bullets aimed at him from the woods. Any sane man would cut his losses in the game, get his horse and high tail it over the back trails out of camp and onto the road to Prescott, or even for Flagstaff. That's what any sane man would, but was Shipley Hart a sane man?

Chisholm waited and watched, his ears tuned to the slightest non-natural noise from the barracks. By the Big Dipper clock it was an hour before midnight when the back door opened. A shadowy figure stepped out carrying a rifle, a pack of some sort and a blanket roll. The man was in a traveling mood. Two more men appeared behind him and they all moved toward the small corral. One of them was Hart, he was sure, only which one? He had to wait until he was certain. The men slipped up on the guard who was not to be surprised the second night in a row. He called out loudly to them, then fired once in the air. Wade heard a brief struggle, then heard the gate swing open and leather creaking as saddles were quickly fastened on. Two minutes later three riders came out of the corral and headed south. The guard sent two shots after them in futile protest.

Chisholm trotted along behind the horses. He could smell them. As they turned from the valley into the woods, he caught a flash of jangling metal. They turned away from the road, not toward it. The road guards would be much more alert than those at the corral, and the deserters knew it. Chisholm established the general direction of the three and guessed that they would not travel more than two or three miles tonight. He debated whether to follow them in the darkness, then decided the risk was too great.

He would establish their general direction for certain and return to his hideout, get his food, his horse and be ready to pick up their trail with first light. It would be a chase, a ride of vengeance.

He trotted with the ten pound Spencer rifle across his chest through the edge of the valley and up the slope toward his knoll.

It took him two hours to get his small pack, find the horse which had strayed a few hundred yards and ride back to the break in the valley where the riders had headed north.

To the north were the higher peaks. The riders were not heading back for Prescott. The rebels had too many agents there. Chisholm sat on his horse and pondered the situation. He could guess where the riders were headed, work up this finger valley and move slowly, watching for a fire, sniffing for smoke. He might run into them in a half dozen miles. Or he could wait until morning and try to stay ahead of the trackers from the rebel camp.

He was sure the rebels would come after the deserters. They wouldn't know why they had run, and would expect spies and worse.

Yes, there would be a tracking force from the camp.

That made up his mind. He had to move on. He checked the lay of the land, the longest finger valley leading around the rebel camp lay directly ahead, slanting almost due north. The Big Dipper pointed at the two o'clock mark around the North Star as he began working slowly ahead. The trail would be easy to follow come morning, but for now, he could only guess.

He rode for two hours, came to the head of the valley and a low pass that led to a ridge that meandered north east. Flag was over that way. He scanned the back trail looking for a fire, trying to catch the first smell of smoke. There was nothing. The half Chiricahua decided that Hart had not let them build a fire. He knew how easily it could give away an otherwise hidden position.

Chisholm got off his horse, ground-tied it and leaned against a tree. He wouldn't sleep, it was too big a chance to take. Instead, he thought through his vengeance ride. It was nothing he had planned. When he saw Hannah lying there, so young with strangulations marks on her white throat, he became a man with one purpose: he would see her killers dead. He still felt the

108

same way. The rebel camp below might be a real problem for the government, a threat maybe even to President Grant, but that was not his first priority. When Shipley Hart was singing his own death song, then Chisholm would think about the rebels.

Morning came slowly, the first light piercing the darkness shyly, then sudden streaks of dawn and at last full light. When he could see the tracks he would be in the area he considered most likely for the trail. It took him half an hour to find the tracks, three shod horses moving slowly up the grade. He had been right. The tracks were less than a day old. His men were heading for Flagstaff or the long way around to get to Prescott.

There were no distinguising marks on the shoes, at least none he could see in the soft footing of the forest floor. He looked back. Far below he saw a group of horsemen moving up the same trail he was on. He would have to discourage them, but not until they got closer.

Chisholm moved out at a faster pace, wondering if the three men ahead had spotted him yet and had a surprise set up for him ahead. Probably. He came to a high meadow and raced across it ignoring the tracks, guessing where they would come out and working along the edge of the grassland for two or three minutes before he noted the tracks. He had gained another five minutes. He wondered what Hart had told his two travelers. They would be the innocents. It was only Hart he wanted; the trouble was the other two men would probably defend him. Chisholm would explain, if there was any time to explain.

He kept working forward, riding as hard as he could yet still keeping the trail. Twice he lost it and had to circle ahead, but he found it again easily. The men were not trying to disguise the trail in any way, but he had the idea that they were riding hard, perhaps hoping for fresh horses unaware that there were few horses anywhere between here and Flagstaff.

Chisholm kept riding. At noon he stopped to give his horse a rest. He had chosen well, she was sturdy and had good wind. At the present rate she would need a rest tonight. He had hopes of catching Shipley Hart before then.

After a long chew on some beef jerky for lunch, he resumed riding. He came upon a pair of boulders in the trail and hesitated. That may have saved his life. Two pistols fired at him and he dove off his mount and bellied up against the rocks.

CHAPTER 8
THE CHIRICAHUA
TROT

The pistols in front of him kept firing, and at first he couldn't figure out why. The slugs were not coming at him. Then he heard the horse scream and she went down. A moment later there was the sound of two sets of hoofbeats as the attackers rode away.

Wade was up and around the rocks quickly, in time to see a bay and a brown horse vanishing around a bend in the trail. Both were being ridden hard.

He looked at his horse. She had gone down. Blood smeared her head and one side. She whimpered, then screamed in terror. Four of the heavy .44 slugs had hit her but had not killed her. She was beyond hope. Wade took his own .44 and shot her once in the head, ending her misery. Then he stripped the rifle from the scabbard, took the extra rounds from the saddle bag and left the loaf of bread and half the beef jerky. He tied the revolver holster down to his leg and shouldered the ten pound rifle. He was ready to move. His tribe had boasted that a Chiricahua brave could make as good time as a troop of mounted cavalry. The only difference was the brave was on foot. Now in the mountains Wade knew he would have a slight advantage. Their horses were tired but he was fresh.

He brought the rifle to port arms in front of him and ran down the trail at the Chiricahua trot, a pace he could keep up for ten or twelve hours. From experience he knew his rate of travel was about seven miles an hour. The heavy rifle would slow him down, but it could be the deciding factor. It was plain to him that the three men ahead had no rifles, otherwise he would be dead. They had tried to bushwhack him with pistols, always a dangerous move against an armed man.

He watched the trail as he ran. The hoofprints evened out now; the fast riding was over. The three riders moved up the trail deliberately, their horses walking. If they continued this pace he should overtake them in an hour and would see them before that.

An hour later the trail was still climbing and he hadn't seen the riders ahead. They rode fast for a mile, slowed to let their mounts rest, then rode again. Hart was a smart, wily fugitive — probably had outdistanced many possees that way. Chisholm bent and examined some horse droppings. He was still an hour behind them. The trail moved downward now, angling back toward the main road to Flagstaff. It would be easier if he could catch them before they gained that road.

Chisholm stopped now and leaned the rifle against a tree. He looked ahead, guessing at the path they would take through the trees. For a moment he caught a flash of yellow below, then it came again through the pines and he saw the rider. They had turned, heading straight for the road. By charging straight down the hill and aiming for a point ahead, he guessed he could overtake them. The trees were thicker here with more brush. The horses would have to slow.

Wade grabbed the rifle and plunged downward, running harder now, making up lost time, knowing that if he beat them to the short rise this side of the road, he would have a good chance at Hart.

The underbrush grabbed at him. A branch slashed him in the face bringing tears where the leaves had scratched his eye. He ran on.

He held the heavy rifle in front of him like

a battering ram to knock aside the branches. His lungs began to burn. Chisholm slowed a little. At the bottom of the ravine he paused for a drink of water, then hurried on. A six point buck jolted out of the brush in front of him and bounded away in twenty foot leaps.

Chisholm struggled up the next ravine, changed his angle and ran hard again, much faster than his seven miles per hour rate. He could never keep up this pace for ten hours.

Twenty minutes later he came to the slope he had seen before. He inspected the open hillside where he had expected the riders to come down. There was nothing. He sighed and looked again, then sat down next to a tree. If he had missed them he would have to get a horse and follow. The trio would drive their mounts to the very limit — kill them before they would go easy on the horseflesh and be captured.

Then he spotted movement out of the timber. Three horses left the brush and crossed the open space. He wasn't sure which one was Shipley Hart, but typically, he would be leading. He wouldn't take the risk of killing the wrong man, so Chisholm lay down on the ridge and sighted in on the horse. A heart shot would be easier, but at

200 yards he had to chance a head shot. The horse kept moving its head for several seconds, then lowered it a little. It set a pattern. The next time the horse dropped its head he was primed and aimed. He fired.

The sudden crack of the Spencer and the jolt of the rifle butt against his shoulder came as a shock after so much stillness. The slug arrived before the sound did, caught the horse below the eye and killed it instantly. It went down and the rider went over its head. The other two riders spurred for the brush just above them and safety.

"Wait for me you sons-of-bitches!" the downed rider screamed.

Wade grinned. He recognized Hart's voice. He had a chance. Chisholm worked the trigger guard lever pumping another round into the chamber. He sent it after the two riders entering the brush, aiming over them.

Then he put another round near Hart. The man had slithered behind the bulk of the dead horse.

Chisholm stood and waved the rifle at Hart. "Shipley Hart, you're a dead man. You can have it fast, or you have it slow. Choose your poison."

The only answer from the downed horse position was a round from Hart's pistol which fell halfway to Chisholm. Wade ran forward, skirting the brush line, moving to cut off Hart from his closest cover.

In a burst of speed, Hart was up and running for the brush.

Chisholm stopped and aimed carefully. He fired, levered another round in and fired again. The second slug caught one of Hart's thighs and he dove into the grass and bushes of the slope. Chisholm moved through the brush again to a position behind a tree and watched Hart. He didn't move. He was playing possum. Chisholm ran for the next tree and before he reached it, a shot thundered behind him. At once his shoulder jolted and burned and he tumbled to the ground. He crawled behind a log and looked behind him.

Wade saw no one in the brush.

"Whoever just shot back there, this is a private affair. Shipley Hart killed my woman. Now I'm gonna kill him. You stay out of it. I could have killed you five minutes ago. I didn't. You're free and clear, now get out of here."

"We're riding with him," a voice answered.

"You don't even know him. He's an outlaw killer, a mad dog, a blight on humanity. Now clear out or I'll kill you, too."

He heard whispering, then brush rattled

and the movement faded away.

His shoulder ached, his left one. He eased around the log and looked toward the meadow.

Shipley Hart was gone.

Chisholm looked down at his wound. The pistol slug was still in his shoulder, in deep. He would be able to use the arm for four hours, no more. Then he'd have to tie it to his chest. Four hours. Hart. He hadn't run away. He might not even be able to walk, but he'd come at his enemy. Hart would try for a kill of his own. His friends had given him the chance.

Wade dropped to the ground and began looking around, examining every spot of brush, every tree. A sweep around his position disclosed nothing suspicious. Maybe Hart couldn't move far without making noise. In the edge of the brush he would set up an ambush and make Wade walk into it.

For five minutes Wade lay there listening. He heard nothing but birds, some large animal far off, and the soft whispering of the breeze high in the pine trees. Time to move. He couldn't bandage his shoulder. Blood ran down his arm. He ignored it.

Cautiously, without a sound, Chisholm began crawling toward the brush closest to where Hart had been. It was thick there. He moved ten yards but could see no man in the area. He angled to the left, deeper into the woods and moved again, relying on his Indian training, but again he found nothing.

He crawled into the center of the area he thought Hart might use to hide, but found nothing. Either Hart was a magician or he was not as badly wounded as Chisholm had thought. But he wouldn't run away. That fact kept hammering at Chisholm. The man would stand and fight, be rid of one more enemy. It just figured.

Chisholm took another idea and worked it. He moved along the edge of the brush line looking for any sign. There would have to be something unnatural, a bent blade of grass, a crushed leaf, a scuffed ant hill. He found it just past the middle of the proposed search area: Two drops of blood splattered a wide leaf.

Hart was hit, he was bleeding and he was moving. Chisholm paused and listened. Far off he thought he heard a sound, but it could have been a rampaging bear. No man would make that sound in the woods when he was trying to be quiet.

Chisholm paused and looked ahead, found another drop of blood, then a mark that showed one leg was being dragged. Now it

118

was simple. He checked out the area ahead, especially the trees, knowing the coon always went up a tree for safety. He suspected that Hart was starting to feel frightened himself.

Chisholm unbuttoned one of his shirt fasteners and pushed his left hand inside his shirt to give it some support. He could get it out fast enough if he needed to use the rifle.

The blood drops became less frequent, but the leg dragged a little more. Chisholm established a direction. Hart was making for the stage road. There were only two stages on the road a week, one each way. Travelers on horseback were few in number.

Chisholm left the trail and jogged down an open slope, across a small ridge and angled back down another valley. If he were right, he should be ahead of the leg dragging Hart — far enough ahead to plan a surprise for him.

Clouds suddenly shielded the sun. Chisholm studied the slopes again. Yes, he should be angling down about here, staying under cover, moving cautiously but as quickly as possible. Any one running had an advantage over the tracker. The one coming behind had to find the trail and had to be cautious against being surprised into an ambush. It gave the advantage to the man out in front.

Only now Chisholm was out in front. He waited. By noon the man had not appeared. Had Hart fooled him? Had he taken a different angle and already hit the wagon road?

The rain began a half hour later, and Chisholm got up and began a careful approach along the line he thought Hart would have taken. He walked a mile along the wooded slope before he smelled them. He was downwind and the sweat of the horses came through to him clearly. Some said the Apache horse thieves could smell a good horse five miles away. These weren't nearly that far. He moved with more caution now, gliding from tree to tree, working upwind, directly into the smell of the horses and now of men. Three men he guessed. Hart's friends had changed their minds and waited for their fellow deserter.

There was no fire.

The rain kept falling, a gentle drizzle that looked like it might go on all day.

He went a half mile before he heard the voices. They were low, yet disdainful of the kind of secrecy needed for an ambush. Maybe they thought he had given up.

Chisholm slid around a big pine and floated to the next pine. When he peered around it he saw the trio. They were all

120

behind logs, their backs to him, facing the back trail.

Hart was in front, nearest the open space across which he was sure the leg dragging had been accented. The other two men lay with their pistols ready.

Wade moved forward again, silent as a rabbit on a hard rock, and stood behind a pine now less than 30 feet from the last man.

"Hell, he turned back. I got him in the shoulder. I told you that, Sarge. He dropped a lot of blood. Probably half way back to Prescott by now." The speaker was tall and thin, with a whine for a voice. "God damn, but it's getting wet. Let's pull out and ride out of here. It's still a hell of a long way into Flagstaff. And we should get that leg of yours looked at."

"I'll worry about the leg," Hart said. He turned and looked at the other two. "Hate to leave that son-of-a-bitch alive. He's got that rifle and could pick us off from a quarter of a mile away."

"Hell, we'll outride him in an hour and be gone."

"That's what we thought before, remember?" He looked up at the sky. "Gonna rain the rest of the day, that should slow him down no matter where he's headed. We should be half way to Flagstaff by the time he gets back to Prescott." He thought about it. "Yeah, let's travel." He stood, hobbling on his right leg, his left held carefully.

One of the men helped Hart up on the bay, then Hart had out his .45. "Now, stand still, both of you. I told you back in camp I didn't want no company, remember."

"You'd be in a hell of a fix if we hadn't changed our minds and come back, Hart."

"Maybe yes, maybe no. But right now we got a problem. Three men and two horses."

"We ride double," the third man said. He was older, maybe 35, and a little heavy.

"I don't ride double," Hart said, ". . . up to you two."

"That's my horse," the heavier man said. "I ain't riding double."

As he spoke the tall thin man vaulted into the saddle of the other horse and wheeled it around. They both faced the heavy man on the ground.

"What the hell's goin on?"

"You walk," Hart said.

"In a pig's eye, I'll walk!" the man said digging for the six gun at his side. Hart had his gun out and shot the man through the left eye before his gun cleared leather. The body jolted backward, a hand freezing the six gun in a death grip.

The man in the other saddle shook his head. "You killed him for a Goddamn horse?"

"He drew on me. You would have done the same thing."

The thin man grinned. "Yeah, you're right, I would have."

"That's what I thought," Hart said turning the six gun toward the other man. "The fact is I'm going to have to travel fast and I *need* two horses."

He shot the man twice in the chest and watched him jolt off the horse.

Before Hart could move for the reins of the spooked horse, Chisholm called out sharply. "You're covered, Hart. Don't even move a muscle or you're dead."

CHAPTER 9
RAINY REVENGE RIDE

Chisholm knew he could get the rifle up into position. As soon as Hart started to spin to fire, Chisholm would cut him down with a rifle slug in the chest. But the wound in his shoulder crossed him up. He pulled his hand out of his shirt and reached for the front of the rifle to steady it. Only the arm did not respond. He couldn't raise his arm!

Quickly he pushed the ten pound rifle against the pine and tried to get off a shot. Hart had spun on cue and fired three times at the sound, then spurred out of the spot uphill. The rifle bullet went wild when Chisholm got it off. He shook his head and ran to the death scene. Both men were dead.

The spooked horse had stopped a dozen yards away. Chisholm walked toward the horse, talking softly. The head came up, ears pricked. The horse snorted and Chisholm knew it would be alright. He shoved the rifle into the scabbard, not really knowing if he could use it again, then held on with his good right hand and threw his left leg over the saddle. He rode out slowly, watching the ground, following the tracks in the softness of the rain soaked forest floor.

After a half hour Chisholm decided Hart was lost. His trail made no sense. One time he started for the upper ridges, then he swung back toward the stage road that was over the small ridge to their right. Now he was moving up the valley toward a small pass above. Chisholm did not know this area. He had heard it called the Death's Head Pass, and that's all he knew. But he kept tracking the man in the softly falling rain until darkness closed in.

Hart had turned back from the pass, moved onto the slope of the ridge next to the stage road, but never went over the top. Now he was back in the heavily timbered lower slopes of the ridge.

Chisholm had to stop because he couldn't find the trail anymore. There was no logical general direction. The only thing Chisholm could figure out was that Hart had lost so much blood he was semi-conscious, riding by instinct, hanging in the saddle from pure habit rather than conscious intent.

When Chisholm stopped he searched the canyons for a cave, but found none. He huddled under a huge downed pine. A narrow strip under the pine remained dry. He sat there and tried to bandage his left shoulder. The bleeding had stopped. He could barely lift his hand now. He tucked it securely inside his shirt front and buttoned the fasteners to keep it there. The beef jerky from his pants pocket had survived and he chewed on it until it turned sweet in his mouth. He was so wet he felt no urge to find any water to drink.

He had thoughts of getting back on his horse and riding up and down the valley until he found Hart, but he let the idea pass, knowing that it would be a miracle if he found him in the blackness and the rain.

It stopped raining about midnight, he estimated. The clouds blew on past and he slept, not waking until well after dawn. He had been too long without sleep not to appreciate it, even if it did put him behind his quarry.

It was a struggle getting on the horse, but at least both his legs worked. He wondered if Hart could mount his horse, or if he had ever dismounted.

The trail was easy to pick up again. Five hundred yards south he found where Hart had spent the night, evidently both dismounting and getting back up. The trail led toward the road again, and back toward the rebel camp and toward Prescott.

Chisholm felt his frustration mounting. He had been following the man too long. His own shoulder needed attention. He prodded the horse into a trot, then lengthened it out and rode hard down the stage road, watching ahead for any sign of Hart.

By the time he had gone two miles he eased off, and let the horse walk. Had he missed Hart? He checked the tracks and saw his mistake. Hart's tracks were not there. He backtracked until he found where Hart had crossed the road and went up a gully on the far side. Reluctantly, Chisholm followed.

He had passed the first twist in the gully when a pistol shot greeted him. It missed. He jerked the horse back and got out of sight. He slid off his horse. Taking his pistol he moved up to the rocks at the bend of the gully.

Peering around he saw only a jumble of rocks beyond, and he was sure Hart lay among them, waiting.

"Come on out, Hart, you're wounded and half dead as it is," Chisholm called, staying out of sight.

Two more shots answered him. Wade studied the gully for cover. There was nothing to hide behind, to protect him. It was thirty yards to the rock pile. He looked at the sides of the small valley and realized he would never be able to climb them with his bad arm.

He checked the arroyo again. There was one depression where the winter rains had gouged out a deeper water channel. It was low enough to shield him. He checked his gun belt and took out six of the bullets. He fired one shot at the rock pile and before any answer could come he ran for the hole, firing spaced shots until his gun was empty. He dove into the depression and fed the six fresh rounds into the six-gun and checked it. Where to now?

He peered over the edge of the riverbed and a shot slapped through the air an inch over his head. He found rocks in the depression and pushed them up to form a small parapet around the front of his hole. Then he threw a few rocks toward where he thought Hart was.

Nothing. He threw a dozen more fist sized rocks and heard a wail of pain. As he threw the rocks he looked for another move. A large rock almost parallel with the ones concealing Hart was a possibility. He checked his rounds, held his aching right arm close to his chest and rushed from the protection of the depression, firing at the rocks where Hart hid. Two shots came back but went wild. He slid in behind the rock and now could see one of Hart's legs extending behind the rock pile. He reloaded, sighted in on the leg and fired once, hitting it. The scream came loud and clear, and Hart pulled the leg out of sight.

"Give it up, Hart, you're done for. No way you're going to walk away from this one. You've lost your crew, your squad. You don't have any rebel band of cutthroats to help you now."

"I'll call you out, whoever you are," Hart yelled. "Just the two of us and our pistols."

"Why should I, you're the one on trial."

"You've killed too, at least two of my men. A face down. Are you afraid?"

"Apache style, with knives."

"No, whiteman style with six-guns."

There was a long-tiredness in Chisholm. It had been too long since he had seen a pretty girl smile, since he had put his head down without having to wonder if it would be shot off the next second. A long-tiredness that he had had enough with for a while. Now there was an urgency to get it over with, one way or the other.

Why not? If he couldn't take out a half-dead bushwhacking woman killer, a rebel crazed killer, then what good was he to anyone else?

"Can you stand up, Hart?"

"I'll stand, if you agree. Man to man. Agreed before we show ourselves, man to man. A matter of honor. In the open. Both with our six-guns in our holsters."

Again he thought why not? But he had the man dead to rights. Another hour and he would be unconscious by the sound of his voice. Why not just wait? No, he was tired. He wanted it finished.

"All right, Hart, you murdering bastard. Anytime you're ready. My six-gun is in my holster. I have no other weapon. Both hands in plain sight, agreed?"

"Agreed. We stand where we are, then either man can go for it first, or we can walk toward each other."

"Right, Hart. Are you ready?"

"Ready."

"Then let's stand up, now." Wade rose slowly, waiting to see the other man's head. It came and they both stood, hands empty hanging at their sides. Chisholm had taken his useless left hand and put it at his side where it hung normally. He stood, feet slightly apart, his eyes glued on Hart's face, then his hands. His face showed pale against the soft sunlight. His clothes dirty, but the gunbelt hung low and tied down.

Sweat beaded Hart's forehead. He started to move his legs, then stopped. For a moment he teetered to one side, then straightened.

"Anytime, hotshot," Hart said.

Chisholm felt his neck muscles tense. He had never been in a stand down like this before. Never. An Apache knife fight was easier. He tensed, then let his right arm relax. He'd always said in a case like this he'd be the first to start the draw, maybe get a slight advantage on the other man.

He did now, his gun hand darting upward, grabbing the hickory handle, lifting the weapon out and up, raising the muzzle and all in one smooth move pulling the trigger, aiming more his arm than the weapon itself.

In the blur of the movements he saw Hart's hand flow upward, saw the gun come out and the muzzle level at his chest, but it didn't fire. His own round caught Hart deep in the belly, threw him to one side and down, rolling him over once. A shriek of pain and fury resounded. The six-gun slid out of Hart's hand.

Chisholm felt a trickle of wetness run down his nose and drip off. He blinked salty sweat out of his eyes and walked forward slowly, the six-gun still ready to fire again.

Hart looked up and shook his head, his hands holding his belly.

"No need for that, it's over. Caught me a bit low, it's harder that way, but just as sure. Tore me up terrible down in there."

Chisholm knelt down beside the man, holstered his weapon and looked at him.

"Hannah Miller," Chisholm said.

"Never heard of her."

"You raped her and then killed her back in Phoenix a week ago."

"Berger did the killing."

"You were there, you're just as guilty."

"You took out Berger and Carlyle?"

"Yes, and you're payment number three."

"You come a hell of a long way to get me."

"Not far, considering the distance Hannah Miller has to go."

"Thought I lost you five, six times. You're one hell of a tracker." He blinked and seemed to concentrate looking closer at Chisholm. "I'll be damned, you're part Breed. No wonder you stuck to me like glue." He grimaced, shut his eyes and shivered. "Would you mind? Man likes to die in peace, alone."

Chisholm got up and walked away, stood there a while, then went and got his horse. When he rode back to where Hart lay, the sleek gunman was nearly dead but hung on long enough to have his last say.

"I beat you, Breed. Do you know that? Look at my six-gun. It's empty. I ran out of firepower, but I beat you. I had your chest centered and the hammer fell before you fired. You were dead and you didn't know it." He tried to smile. "So what the hell, one way's as good as another. It don't matter man, not when you're gonna die."

Chisholm didn't have to check the empty revolver, he believed Hart. He'd seen the muzzle come up fast, terribly fast. He looked back down at Hart and saw his eyes go glassy, open and look at the sun without squinting. There was an angry painful twisting of his face. Chisholm nodded.

"That's three, Hannah," he said softly. Mounting, he nudged the horse into a walk and rode back to the stage road.

He urged the mount along faster for a while, not sure how far out of Prescott he was nor how well he could sit the saddle. Now and then a dizzy spell hit him. He couldn't have lost that much blood. With a little luck he should get back to Prescott before noon, and if not then, by supper. Come to think of it he was hungry. He'd argue old sawbones Doc Crowder to pull that rebel bullet out of his shoulder and maybe rest up for a few hours. He should be able to trade that to General Crook for the information about the rebel company up the road to Flag. Yes, he should be able to do that.

CHAPTER 10
EVEN STEVEN TRADE:

Chisholm lay looking up at the ceiling, and suddenly realized that he was awake and alive, and that he really was in the army hospital at Camp Prescott. He turned to the private sitting near him and scowled.

"When do we eat around here," Chisholm growled.

The soldier jumped in surprise, nodded and left the room. A few moments later he was back with Doctor Crowder who looked at his shoulder, the frown easing a little.

"When you sleep, Chisholm, you sleep like a bear in February. How the hell do you feel?"

"Ready to ride. What time is it?"

"Past seven in the evening. I've told General Crook that you're awake, but not rational. You haven't been rational since Swallow River Camp, and I can't say I blame you. Anyway he'll be over here in a few minutes.

"You realize you busted in on my supper last night, fell off your horse and passed out on the steps. All we could get out of you was "the Rebels are here," then you'd pass out again. General Crook is damned anxious to know what you meant. He just got word that President Grant is going to be in Denver shortly and all federal troops are supposed to be on the alert."

"Denver is 800 miles from here."

"So, guns have horses, you know."

Before he could reply, General Crook came in and stared down at Wade.

"Chisholm, now maybe you'll make yourself clear. What the hell is this about rebels? I thought we'd seen the last of them back in Sixty-Five."

"That rebel slug should prove otherwise, General," Chisholm said. Then he went on to tell the General and the doctor what he had learned at the old mine a few miles outside of Prescott.

"How many men?" Crook asked.

"I didn't get a count, but one of them said 150."

"And mobile. Did every man have a horse?"

"I only saw about twenty, but I figured each soldier who answered the call would come riding in on one of his own. I'd say they could move."

"Then we better start doing the same."

"I'm with you," Chisholm said.

The doctor frowned. "You're not getting out of that bed, soldier. You need at least two days of rest."

"Cut it out, Doc. I'm Chiricahua, remember. Any Apache brave who can't fight with one good hand is put out in the desert to breathe dust, didn't you know that?" Chisholm sat up, steadied himself against the doctor and smiled at the General. "See, I'll be ready to ride in an hour. How many men are you taking?"

"They'll fight?"

"You'll have to fight your way in. I'd say half will stand and fight and half melt into the hills."

"We'll work out a two pronged attack. As soon as you get some clothes on, report to my headquarters." Crook watched him, pulled at his full beard that flared out in two points which earned him the Indian nickname of Fork-beard. But his eyes were compassionate. He watched Chisholm again and nodded. "You take it slow, son, there's no rush. Them Rebs been sitting there for months from what you say, they won't be moving out in a day."

Doctor Crowder stared at his patient.

"Lift your left arm, Chisholm. I'm going to tape your left arm across your chest, and you damn well better leave it there."

With his arm taped, Chisholm tried to get into the heavy brown pants.

"Want some help?" asked the Doc.

Chisholm glared at him as he tried to get into his pants with one hand.

Doc Crowder laughed. "Yeah, I know, any Apache brave. . . . What does that mean about breathing dust? I never did know."

"You didn't? Paleface! In most Indian cultures anyone who can't work and be productive to the tribe is not considered a member of the tribe. Except for the very small children, everyone works. When an old brave, or an old woman can't work, that individual is sent into the desert alone. She usually starves to death in a few days and that way is not a burden on the hard pressed tribe."

"You people are tough, aren't you? What about a brave who is cut up badly, so wounded he can't fight anymore?"

"If a brave can't fight, he's no longer a warrior. If he can't work, he's no longer a man, and he too is turned out to breathe the desert dust."

The general had left, and now the Doctor moved toward the door.

"Well, Wade, all I can say is I'm glad you're only half Chiricahua. I won't even tell you to take it easy." He paused. "Oh, before you get on a horse, you'd better practice loading that .44 of yours with one hand. It's a little tricky." He paused. "Better yet, draw another .44 so you can ride with two of them loaded. It just might save your contrary red hide."

Chisholm looked after him, and grinned.

The troops were on the trail the next morning at 3 a.m. Together, General Crook and Wade had worked out a plan. A token force of some fifty men, all mounted, would strike at the front gate, smash through and charge down the road alerting all the guards.

The main force would be coming up from the south through the valley and strike directly at the Ranch house and the barracks. Four hundred men would form a line of skirmishers and ride into the fray as soon as the first troop had punched into the gate and drawn off some of the troops. The time of the attack would be six a.m. Lieutenant Josh Donner would lead the strike at the gate with half of B company.

He and Wade rode out ahead to find the exact location of the gate. When they spotted the gate, Wade rode hard back down the

Prescott road to the turnoff, met the men and led the main body of four hundred cavalrymen through the mountains to where he could see the valley and the Ranch house in the distance. The Rebels had no security at all to the south.

"I would suggest no bugles, sir," Wade said to General Crook. "The bugle lets the enemy know exactly who is coming. If we sweep in, the element of surprise will be doubled. They might think it's part of an early morning exercise. We should over-run them before they can find their ammunition and fire a shot."

"Right, Chisholm, no bugles on the attack. Each unit will keep eye contact with the rest. When Captain Chisholm moves out, the rest of us charge with him."

"Captain hell!" Wade said with a grin. "Last time we had our little talk, you gave me an oak leaf."

General Crook laughed. "True, but I took it back. Call me an Indian giver."

Wade laughed and watched the sky lighten and bleed into dawn. It wouldn't be long now. He estimated the road gate where Lieutenant Donner would attack was less than two miles away. Moments later he heard rifle shots in the stillness of the morning air. A dozen, maybe 18, reports came, and General Crook had his field glasses up watching the buildings. They couldn't wait much longer.

Various groups of men had been assigned to specific buildings. Upon breaking through, anyone inside would be killed or captured and the area secured.

"I think it's time we move, sir," Wade said. "No bugles." Wade lifted his six-gun, saw the officers down the line lift their sabres, and a moment later the four hundred men swung across the valley at a trot. When the line straightened, they picked up speed and the last quarter of a mile they were in a full gallop as they streamed toward the buildings.

Wade had seen no one yet. Were they all sleeping, or at mess call? At last one lone blue uniformed man came from the Ranch house, looked at the charging blue coats, and scurried back inside.

A shot came from a broken window in the Ranch house, then another. Scattered reports came from the other structures as the units fanned out into the various buildings.

Wade and General Crook charged into the Ranch house behind half a dozen troopers. They found only four blue clad rebels and some burned papers, the remains of a command. Nothing more. One of the rebels inside had been shot in the face when he raised his rifle to fire. The other three surrendered. General Crook stood in front of one, his eyes glaring.

"Where is the rest of your command?" he bellowed.

"Gone, sir."

"Gone where, damn you?"

The blue clad man remained silent.

"You'll say, you rebel spy, or I'll cut your throat, you understand me?" Crook's eyes bulged, his beard shook and he seemed like the devil himself.

"Left last night sir, on the trail to Flagstaff."

"Where are they going from there?"

"To Denver, sir."

Rifle fire erupted outside and then tailed off. Crook looked back at the rebel prisoner. "You know I should shoot you right here out of hand. You're a spy, a rebel, a usurper. You have no rights, none whatsoever." He motioned to Lieutenant Johnson, his aide. "See that all prisoners are tied, roped together and marched back to Prescott. Take a detail of as many men as you need. Then get a report immediately about the situation in the other buildings."

As he spoke Captain Barr came in.

"Sir, we've secured the remaining buildings. We found only twenty odd men. Lt. Donner said there were only two men at the gate. They were killed. He suffered one wounded. We have two more wounded, none seriously."

Outside General Crook kept pulling at his beard. "If they left last night they can't have more than a six or eight hour head start. We form up and move out as soon as possible, Captain Barr. Get us moving for Flag. We'll pursue and capture."

Barr saluted and ran into the camp shouting orders. Five minutes later they had formed up into a long column of twos and were riding out toward the road gate. The twenty three prisoners would be returned to Prescott by four troopers. Two more would remain to dig six graves for the dead, then rejoin the troop on march.

Wade rode up beside General Crook in the center of the column.

"General Crook, sir, I know a general class officer is only a few steps from the almighty himself, but you were jolted out of your skin when that reb said the troop was marching for Denver. Why?"

"You know that, Chisholm. President Grant is going to be in Denver within three weeks. I told you about the alert. The Pinkertons think somebody may try to kill Grant while he's in Denver. And from what you've told me about this motly crew, they may be the ones who will try."

"To assassinate President Grant?"

"What more would give the southern rebel element a thrill?"

"Now how do we catch them?"

"I've ordered six men ahead. Each is a scout and a sharpshooter, and each man has two horses. They are to move at a gallop, alternating horses, and try to make a sighting of the rebel force. A hundred and thirty men are hard to hide. They must be moving openly, but it's my guess they will go around any towns they come to, especially any with a lawman or a telegraph wire."

"The extra horses you liberated from the Rebels?"

"Exactly. You're sounding more like a major all the time."

"I'd like to go with the scouts."

"Denied. You're on limited duty, even for a Chiricahua."

"What's their actual lead time over us?"

"From what my officers tell me, the prisoners claim the troop left anywhere from darkness last night to about midnight. Say ten p.m. It's now seven a.m. They have a nine hour lead."

"So if we force march it, and lope for an hour, then walk for an hour, we can average five miles an hour. We should gain one mile an hour on them."

"But they're 40 miles ahead of us."

"So, we've got a problem," Wade said. He thought about it. "Maybe I can help. Listen through and then start yelling. This is what I suggest."

A halfhour later Wade had his arm tape cut away. He put the arm into his shirt. He could use it a little. Maybe with use, it would get stronger.

He was on a gray with a remuda of three horses on a rope behind him. Four more men were so equipped, the extra horses running free without saddles, only bridles. Each man had rations for two days, hardtack and jerky, and a canteen of water. The four men were all volunteers, all marksmen, and all had repeating Spencer's and 200 rounds of ammunition. Over the road, Wade reasoned that a good horse could travel ten miles in an hour, then for five minutes they would wipe down the mount, and saddle the next mount in line, adding the winded horse to the end of the remuda. Then ride for another hour at the ten miles per hour galloping pace.

Wade figured the rebels had at most a 25-mile lead. They wouldn't force march it. There were no telegraphs in the mountains of Arizona so there was no way to wire ahead that they were in trouble. A four horse rider team was the only way. And at Clarkdale, Wade would take the cutoff that used to go to the Clarkdale mine. He could chop off five miles of roadway by that maneuver. He was sure the strangers would not know about the shorter route. The way he figured it, his team should be catching up with the rebels at the rate of almost six miles an hour. At that rate they should catch them before sundown. From there on he would play it the way it fell.

They caught the other scout team during the second hour. Wade instructed them to forge on ahead as planned, and when they made contact with the rebels to take cover and attack their rear guard. That would be enough to harrass them. By then Wade figured he and his team would have passed them and set up a road block ahead. At least that was the plan.

They rode the second hour, wiped down the horse and saddled up. Chisholm had help moving his saddle. His arm hurt more now, and he slid it inside his shirt to rest it. He was leading the team and had just come

146

around a bend when his horse shied as a ruffled grouse took off from the road, sounding like a sudden thunderstorm with the roaring of its wings. The horse stepped on a rock, its foreleg snapped and the horse went down, throwing Chisholm over its head. He hit on his left shoulder, shouted in agony at the fury of the pain and passed out even before he stopped rolling.

CHAPTER 11
FIRE AND FALL BACK

By the time the first trooper dismounted and got to him, Wade had come back to consciousness and sat up. He held his shoulder, shaking his head to beat back the pain.

"Are you hurt?" the soldier asked.

Wade snorted. "What a hell of a question to ask. I always sit on my fanny looking up at the trees."

As he finished saying it, a pistol cracked in the silence. He looked at his horse. It kicked once more and then was quiet.

"Get the saddle off her and on the next one, we can't sit around here all day." He chewed some jerky as he watched them saddle his next horse. The man with the pocket watch said they were halfway through the hour. Wade decided this horse would have to last for an hour and a half.

When the horse was ready he got to his feet. At least his legs still worked. Each step exaggerated the grinding pain in his shoulder. He didn't want to think what the jolting of a gallop would feel like. But he felt it a few seconds later.

Chisholm simply thought about something else. The cutoff to the Clarkdale mine came up and he studied the path a hundred yards off the road. No large group of riders had passed that way in six months. It spurred him on and they rode. They were almost back to the main road when their hour was up.

Wade wiped down his mount, but left the saddle on. He checked over the last two mounts left in his remuda. Both had been ridden now. Both were rested but not fresh. He wasn't sure if they each could go an hour at a time with a rider. He might have to cut the gallop period to five miles. And they might come near the rear guard of the rebels before then. He figured they were thirty miles down the road. Three hours. The rebels should still be seven or eight miles ahead. They should catch them in the fifth hour.

They were riding again.

Wade held the gallop to a little slower pace than he had so far, and his horse seemed to be weathering it well. They were on a downslope in the mountains, working along the stage road with a four mile straight stretch spread out ahead of them along the side of a slope and then across a three mile long valley. At the foot of the slope he saw them.

The rebels were stopped. No dust rose from their company. Wade reined in his team and showed them. Without a word they moved on. The rebels would be across the valley before Wade and his team could get there. Unless they were stopped for a long break. It was nearing noon. Perhaps a hot meal for the troops, Wade hoped.

His plan had come from the situation. He would go down the stage road as far as possible, then cut around the near side of the valley staying under cover, hoping to beat the rebels to the stage road where it entered the far stretch of timber. At that point they could put up a road block, catch the rebels in the open and, hopefully, discourage them from advancing. There would be no help from the rear for six to eight hours, even if the four men could hold. The terrain could have been better, a mountain pass, or a steep walled canyon would have been better. Fate didn't deal that way this time.

Now the men rode flat out, urging every bit of power from the sturdy army mounts. They had to move slower in the woods as they circled the valley itself. To their surprise the rebels had not moved from their lunch camp. Evidently, they thought they were far enough ahead, either that or no rear guard action had been reported.

A mile from the end of the woods' ride, Wade had to change horses. The others did too, and they came to their hoped for spot before the enemy began to move. With the horses, they dragged four downed logs across the trail, then put their horses well to the rear and found defensive positions where they had good fields of fire.

Then they waited.

Chisholm spread out his ammunition in front of him and rested the repeating Spencer between the two logs that formed his firing position. Ridiculous. Militarily the position was untenable. Four men against 130! And no good defensive positions and no flank protection. They should be either overrun or outflanked in the first five minutes.

But only if the rebels knew who was opposing them. They had worked out a systematic fire and move plan, with the two men on the outside firing and moving out twenty yards, firing, then moving another twenty yards and firing.

The effect could look like a spread of over

200 yards of dug in troopers firing at the oncoming force.

He hoped it would work.

There had been little time to plan anything else. The troops were coming now less than a mile away. They seemed to be in a column of fours, with a lead man. A one man point! They would let the lead men get past them, then kill him and the rest fire on the column at a range of no more than 50 yards. With any luck the surprise attack would confuse the front ranks, turn them and send them flying back into the valley and out of range.

They waited another ten minutes, then the advance man was nearing the fringes of brush. The other center man was assigned to hit the point man as Chisholm scanned the troops, looking for the man who seemed to be in charge. The only prospect he could see was a man riding to the right of the column and slightly ahead of the main party. An officer of some kind. He sighted in on the officer. The second he heard the first shot near him he fired as well. The officer plunged from his horse, and Wade swung his Spencer to the main body. They fired at the first four men in line, then shot at the horses' heads. Soon four animals were down and threshing in the line of march. The troops screamed. Some turned, wheeling mounts and riding to the left and right. Many turned in place and spurred backwards, out of danger. The rifles kept firing at them, but there was no return fire.

Either the men were too shocked to return fire or they had not loaded their weapons. It was over in 45 seconds. The last shots came from the wooded area and most of the rebels had panicked and retreated. In front of them lay six horses, dead or dying, and seven men Chisholm could count on the ground.

The rest of the troop had spurred a half mile away into the center of the valley and stood in a confused mass. One or two men seemed to be trying to restore order.

Chisholm whistled and the man closest to him ran hard back into the brush for the best four horses they had left. Each man mounted and waited. There would be no chance to repeat their performance. They would delay them here and then mount, sniping attacks on the troop as it moved forward. If it moved forward. There was a chance now that they would break up into small units and proceed to their assigned locations for the conspiracy. At least that's what they should do.

Chisholm was glad to see that he was wrong. Ahead he saw the men formed into

153

a line of skirmishers and now riding hard for the woods. Two of the men rode into the woods and brush. They would ride until they were well to each side of the line of skirmishers and let the men pass uncontested. Even before they had cleared the road area, shots began coming. Lead whizzed through the trees as they rode hard to the side.

Chisholm and a trooper named Clark sat on their mounts and let them blow on a small rise out of the path of the rebels. The long line of horsemen had not wavered. It had rushed into the woods, past the road block, and stopped. Several men went back to check the dead, and that was when Chisholm realized that the rebels did not have on their light blue uniforms. They all wore civilian clothes. They were implementing their plot.

He and Clark left their horses and crawled within two hundred yards of the troops. Most of them milled around just inside the trees, waiting orders.

They lay down on the rise and sighted in. Before they could open fire, he heard shots from the other side and nodded. The other two bluecoats were at work.

Clark and Chisholm fired fourteen rounds each into the churning mass of troops and horses, jumped up and ran for their own mounts as they saw a six man team break off from the group below and charge toward them. Clark and Chisholm rode hard, slanting to the front in an arc, putting themselves well out of reach of the angry rebels. They paused on another small rise and saw the six riders below give up the chase. As the riders moved back to the main party, Chisholm and Clark shadowed them. The rebels had not moved from their position inside the woods. They were digging graves. Chisholm couldn't believe it! In the middle of a fight they stop to dig graves. Maybe they thought the battle was over.

The sun showed the time was about four in the afternoon when Chisholm and Clark heard firing from the far side of the group. That could be the Spencers from the other two bluecoats. They saw a squad ride off in pursuit. Chisholm waited for fifteen or twenty minutes, then they fired on the group again, sending seven shots each into the troops, then riding away fast as a contingent came after them.

They circled the opposite way this time, throwing off the chasers.

Clark had the pocket watch.

"Ten minutes after four," Clark said responding to Chisholm's question. "I figure every hour we stall them here is worth five to six miles for the main body."

"And the advance party should be about three hours behind us, maybe four. They could get here before dark. Clark, you swing around the rebels below and go up the way we came through the timber and around the valley. Maybe you can make contact with that advance group. When you do bring them down, put three on each side for more firepower. I hope we can keep these bastards pinned down all night. If we can, Crook will be here by morning. Oh, leave one man on the trail at the far end of the valley to meet Crook."

Clark said he'd do that, saluted, and rode off. Curiously, Chisholm had returned the salute without thinking.

It worked out the way Chisholm guessed. He and the other two bluecoats across the way sent harassing fire into the rebels all night. They fired and moved, and fired again. By morning he sensed a change in the rebels' position. As the light gained he saw why.

General Crook had slid his men into position. Now Chisholm could see a double ring of dug in bluecoats below him not more than 200 yards from the rebels. He moved closer to the edge of the woods and with the full light he heard a series of three pistol shots. General Crook and two aides rode forward from a mass of 200 troopers, carrying a large white handkerchief tied on the end of a sabre. Chisholm worked his way to the very edge of the brush where he could get a better view and hear some of the words.

Crook didn't take long to speak.

"Men in the woods. You're surrounded by members of the 5th U.S. Cavalry. There is no chance to escape. You have dead and wounded. This enterprise is doomed to failure, it is over. I have over seven hundred troopers with rifles aimed at you. Send out your spokesman and surrender."

Wade heard angry voices below in the rebels' camp, then there were two closely spaced shots. In the silence that followed a lone rider left the brush and walked his horse slowly toward Crook. He held his side and seemed in obvious pain.

When he reached the General he held out his rifle to Crook, tried to salute, then fell head first into the tall grass of the valley floor.

Crook let him lay there, signalled his troops to advance and they rode slowly toward the woods in a massed front without a weapon being raised.

It was only then that Wade realized he hadn't been worrying about his shoulder. The sudden acknowledgement of the wound sent searing pains through his upper arm and shoulder and he had to struggle to mount his horse. Then he rode down to the camp of the rebels, anxious to find out why they had not scattered during the night when they had the chance.

He was almost to the group, when he fell forward against the saddle horn and found that he couldn't lift his head. Two troopers saw him and rode beside him so he wouldn't fall off the horse. Wade Chisholm gritted his teeth as he thanked the men with his eyes. Never had he felt such pain.

CHAPTER 12
HANNAH MILLER

Chisholm sat in the hospital bed and winced when Doc Crowder probed into his shoulder.

"Damn fool. I told you to stay here. You have to be the big shot hero. Hell, Crook and his men would have found them without you, and you wouldn't have risked losing that arm."

"It's always fun to talk to you, Doc. Pleasing bedside manner, full of humor and witty sayings."

The doctor didn't respond. He put the medication on the shoulder wound where he had removed the rebel bullet two days before and bandaged it.

"George wants to see you. I told him that generals came second, right after doctors." He sighed. "Well, I guess you'll live until I have to patch you up again." He shook his head. "This time I've got you for three days. Which means I've stolen your clothes.

George said you had to stay until that shoulder straightens out." He frowned and walked out of the room.

General Crook came in a few minutes later.

"The sawbones still mad?"

"Seems to be."

"Well, I'm not angry with you, Chisholm. I got off two dispatch riders this morning to Denver. They should get there in plenty of time to warn the federal people about the rebel group here, on the chance that there are more of them around. I'll bet they take good care of the President."

"Yes sir. General Crook, why didn't they scatter when we hit them in the woods? They didn't know how big a force we had but they must have known there were less than eight or ten of us."

"I asked the same question of their top man, a Colonel Jones, who newly appointed himself. Seems that they lost their ranking leader in that first ambush at the entrance to the woods. After that there were two factions and they almost started fighting among themselves. So they sat there and gave us time to catch them. We made better than six miles an hour for forty-five miles, did I tell you that?"

"That's good time. How many horses did you lose?"

"Sometimes you're too smart for your own good, Chisholm. We lost twelve, which isn't bad for that pace. Not dead, just played out. We picked them up on the way back, but you probably don't remember much of that, you were out of your head part of the time."

"Sorry."

"You don't sound sorry." The General was turning over and over in his hand a gold major's oak leaf. "Have you done any more thinking about this little bobble?"

"Some."

"When you decide, let me know." General Crook pulled at his beard. He walked to the end of the bed, then looked up. "Oh, it seems you made quite an impression on a certain young lady we have in camp. Captain Thornton's daughter is smitten with you."

"You had a talk with her, I hope, about her father?"

"Yes, she told me your idea about convincing him that he should resign for his daughter and wife's sake. Between the two of them they turned the trick. Captain Thornton will be in my office tomorrow morning with his official resignation."

"Then there won't be any court martial,"

Chisholm said.

"Not if we can get the charges withdrawn. Lt. Donner has been on the patrol with us, but I think he'll be glad to withdraw the charges once Captain Thornton is a civilian."

"Good. Now, how are my people doing in the Superstitions?"

General Crook sat down in the chair and stared at Wade. "Things are quiet. I have reports that one rather large band under Two Knife is ready to come in and go to the reservation. We talked about it before. I'd still like you to be my representative to go in and find Two Knife and talk to him."

"I've got this one other little job to do first."

"Hannah Miller? I thought the score was settled."

Wade laughed. "Not much privacy around this end of the territory is there. That was a private affair."

"Then you'll be going back to Phoenix?"

"As soon as I want to fork a horse, regardless of what the old sawbones says."

General Crook stroked his beard, his eyes narrowed and became thoughtful. "Wade, remember that your people need you. There doesn't have to be this constant confrontation. The white man and the Apache can live in peace. There are going to be some adjustments needed on both sides, but for those who can adjust, it will be a good life. We don't have to repeat the Salt Creek Cave affair time after time."

He got up, walked to the window and came back, his face showing a frown. "Don't quote me on any of this. I'm getting a bad enough name for being soft on Indians as it is. If Bill Sherman knew how I'm talking he would probably try to run me back to the Army Headquarters in Washington where I couldn't cause any trouble. The fact is, I know enough about Indians to see them as human beings, not as savages, not as an 'enemy' that must be exterminated. And as you know, that's how most of our top brass feels these days. My pledge to you, Wade. If you'll work with me, I'll do everything I can to see that the Indians are treated fairly."

Wade had watched the general with steady eyes. Now, he nodded. "Thank you, General Crook, I believe you will. And I will hold you to your pledge."

General Crook stood. "Chisholm, you come back and see me when your business down south is finished. I want to get something underway within two weeks at the most." He stared at Wade for a moment, then turned and left the room.

Wade watched him go, smiled and saluted. "Yes, sir, general, sir," he said softly.

Three days later Wade talked Dr. Crowder into releasing him. It was an easy two day ride south and since the stage wasn't running for three more days, he'd ride. He was in his hotel room the day before he left when a knock came shortly after noon time. He went to the door warily. When he opened it, he found Jocelyn Thornton smiling at him.

She walked into the room and motioned for him to close the door. He left it partly open and smiled at her.

"I understand you are quite a persuader," he said.

"Oh, yes, Father. Both mother and I talked to him and pleaded and cried and at last he simply threw up his hands and said he'd retire from the army if it would keep us happy. This noon we had the little ceremony and he's a civilian now. We'll leave on Wednesday's stage."

"Good, that's the best for all of you, especially for your father. You'll like it in Boston."

"You've been there?"

"Yes, a few times."

"Oh, I see. I might not go," she said walk-

164

ing around him and closing the room's door.

"And why wouldn't you go with your parents?"

"I might stay here and get married. I might marry you, Wade Chisholm."

"You might, you say, but I haven't asked you, and anyway you're only sixteen."

"Lots of girls in Prescott marry when they're sixteen."

"That's because there are so few girls in Prescott."

"You're not asking is no problem. I'll ask you."

"You can't do that, Jocelyn, it just isn't done."

"Wade, I don't care much about what is or isn't done. Will you marry me, Wade Chisholm?"

He smiled, made a strange motion with his hand.

She took off her blue, light weight jacket and began unfastening the buttons on the front of her blouse.

"Jocelyn, what in the world. . . ."

"I wouldn't think of asking you to marry me without showing you what I look like."

The blouse was open.

Wade stood there almost too surprised to move. He knew he should not laugh. He walked to her and caught her hands, stopping her.

"Jocelyn, I can't sit here and let you do this. I thought you knew, I'm already married. There's a girl in Phoenix."

"But everyone told me . . . I mean they said you were unmarried."

"People don't know everything about a person, even when they think they do. I'm sorry, Jocelyn, I can't marry you. That wouldn't be fair to any of us, would it?"

Tears came, seeping slowly. She slashed them away, more anger than hurt showing on her face. Slowly she began fastening the buttons again. When she was done he handed her the light blue jacket.

"I'd just as soon you didn't tell anybody about what I told you. It's because I don't want any of my enemies taking out their hatred of me on my wife. You can understand that. If they knew I was married they would kidnap her and then. . . ."

She brushed away the last of the tears. "Yes, Wade, I understand. Now I understand a lot of things." She swallowed, took several deep breaths. "So, now I guess I will be going back to Boston. I was born there, did you know that? So I'll fit right in and there will be dances, and lots of dresses and fancy parties." Jocelyn brushed a white handkerchief at her eyes, then turned toward the

166

door. "And in Boston a proper young lady never is in a gentleman's bedroom with the door closed." She went to the door and smiled, but the dimples didn't come through.

"Goodbye, Mr. Chisholm. Thank you for what you've done for my father, all of us."

She was out the door and gone.

Wade sat down on the bed and slowly shook his head. He was fully aware that he had just been through a close call, one that could have been more dangerous than all of the rebel marksmen.

Two days later he rode into Phoenix. As he tied up his horse outside the McCurdy General Store, he couldn't help but think about the last time he had been tied up here, before he went to see where Hannah was and why she hadn't come to the store that morning. His eyes hardened for a moment. Then he wrapped the reins around the hitching rail and pushed into the dimly lit store.

Josh McCurdy waved from behind the small counter.

"You catch them, Wade?"

"Yes, it's finished, the score evened."

"Good. World's lot better off without their kind living in it. You missed the funeral.

167

Nothing fancy, just a few words by Brother McCall, but all proper."

"You took care of everything?"

"Yes." He looked at the door, then back at Wade. "One quick drink in memory of Hannah Miller. We didn't know her very long, but it was an honor for all of us."

The men tipped the pint whiskey bottle in turn before Josh capped it and put it under the counter.

"Now, to business. You probably forgot when you were here last, that I told you I found something out at the Miller place. I went through the burned out house and found a little cellar under the place. Lots of people do that to hide in if Indians come. In the cellar I found this iron chest with locks on it. Hadn't even told Hannah about it, wanted you here when we looked it over. Now be a good time?"

Wade Chisholm nodded.

Josh carried the eighteen inch long chest by metal handles on each end. It was a foot deep and about that wide, not fancy but of metal thick enough to hold up under a good fire. Josh used a hammer on the padlocks and both popped open with half a dozen whacks.

Wade lifted the cover and they looked at a score of envelopes, most containing papers.

168

Below the envelopes was a glint of gold coins.

"Well now, Wade, it looks like that woman of yours was an heiress of some sort."

It took them most of the rest of the evening to go over what was in the iron box. The papers were some stocks and bonds on Eastern companies, some worth quite a lot of money. In another envelope was a grant deed showing the 640 acres all free and clear and the deed filed with the territorial county recorder.

Josh had stacked the double eagle gold coins and counted them. There were 150 of them . . . three thousand dollars.

Wade totaled up the face value of the stock certificates and lifted his brows. The certificates had an indicated value of more than twenty-five thousand dollars.

Wade looked at Josh. "That's a lot of money."

"Lordy, Lordy, Lordy. It most certainly is. But who does it belong to now?"

"We look for relatives. Those letters, there must be someone close to them. We'll find an address or two on those letters."

After another two hours of scouring the letters they found no indication of relatives. The letters were from friends in the East, Chicago and Philadelphia, but never a note about a parent or brother, about a relative of any kind.

The next morning the problem was just as tough as it had been the night before.

"She was planning on marrying you, Wade. She told me that. Why can't you take the money?"

"Because it isn't mine."

They looked at the papers again, then Wade snapped his fingers.

"Did that half-baked lawyer here in town have you sign any papers when you bought the house for Hannah?"

Josh thought about it, then nodded. "Seems like that young know-it-all lawyer guy said it was a power of attorney. What's that?"

"Let's go see your lawyer friend," Wade said.

An hour later they had it worked out. The man who had read for the law was J. Lawson Ambrose, and he studied the paper he had made out previously. Then Wade presented the problem.

"Impossible, it can't be done. It might have to go all the way to the territorial legislature. It would cost a lot of money."

Wade relaxed. "Now we're getting somewhere, Ambrose. You do exactly as I say, set it up all legal and unbreakable, and you'll get a two hundred dollar fee."

"Make it three hundred."

"Done." Wade said. They took the box of papers with them as they left the office and Josh McCurdy was still a little mixed up about the whole thing.

"You mean you won't take a cent of all that money, Wade?"

"Right."

"And you told Ambrose to set it up as a trust fund that would be used to run a school for orphaned and abandoned kids?"

"That's right, Josh. You've got it."

"And the cash is to build a school house and a ranch house out on the Miller place. I understand you calling it the Hannah Miller School. But you don't get a cent?"

"You have got it. What about a drink?"

"At least that I understand."

"Josh, I've never owned a thing in my life besides a horse and a saddle. What would I do with twenty-five thousand dollars? Probably just lose it. This way, everybody in the state will know the name Hannah Miller, and they'll know all about her and her school. Oh, I forgot to tell you, it's up to you to get the buildings put up and to find a schoolmarm. And remember, the Hannah Miller School is specially for Indian kids and colored kids and Mexican kids. You can

171

throw in some roundeyes, too, just to make it look good."

"Wade, I don't know a damned thing about running a school."

"So start learning, that's what a school is for. Oh, by the way, you get $20 a month as the school's first administrator."

Josh grinned. "Well now, this is sounding better all the time. Where was that drink you were offering?"

Wade got a room at the hotel and took a long hot bath, then dressed and swung up on his horse to ride to the outskirts of the village. He got down at the gate and walked among the graves until he found the newest one with a small wooden cross on it labeled Hannah Miller.

He knelt down by her grave and looked at the mound of dirt for a long time — thinking what might have been, what should have been. How delightfully happy she had been the few days they were together.

Then he got up and rode back to the store. Josh should have his bedroll and supply pack ready. He was going into the Superstition Mountains for a week to rest and recuperate, Indian style. Then he would ride to Prescott again and have a long talk with General George Crook. A lot of his people were still up in the mountains, and they didn't know who to believe. He had to go in and talk to them.

That made him think about the gold oak leaves and the myriad of responsibilities and connotations that went with them. He would think about the offer, but right now, he didn't think he would ever be back in the army again. It would depend on how he could best help his people.

"The moons would come and the moons would go, but the great Apache nation would last forever!" His mother used to tell him that. The medicine doctor had told the tribe that. But the white man had never said it.

Perhaps he was the link between the Indian and the white that could help save his people, help teach them to live at peace with the white man, to take the best the white culture could offer and blend it with the best of the Indian. Who knew both sides better than he?

Perhaps.

A week in the Superstitions would give him time to think.